A Brand N  ling

The Donut Shop Mysteries

The Classic Diner Mystery Series
Book 1

A CHILI DEATH
by
Jessica Beck

To my family,
for giving me their unconditional support over the years,
even in the most trying of times!

Chapter 1

First things first.

I didn't kill Howard Lance.

Just because I'd been the one who found him dead in the deep freezer at my family's café, The Charming Moose Diner, didn't mean that I had anything to do with it, and neither did my husband, Greg. At first, nobody was pointing any fingers at him, though. Before we'd narrowed down Howard's time of death, it appeared that my husband had what must have been the best alibi in the state of North Carolina; on the evening of the murder, Greg was playing poker with the sheriff, the mayor, the head of our local church's building fund, an auto mechanic, and the town barber. There wasn't a soul in all of Jasper Fork, North Carolina who would dispute the words of that collection of solid citizens.

Me? I wasn't so lucky. Greg had left the diner at six, a full hour before we normally locked the doors for the night. Mom came back one night a week to cover the last hour of the kitchen while we were open, and we always had fun working together. After we closed that night and Mom went home, I'd decided to stay behind, intent on updating the inventory in our freezer while my husband had his weekly night out with the boys. After all, there was no reason to hurry home to an empty house. Still, I didn't begrudge my husband his poker games. Working and living together made for close quarters sometimes, and we needed a break from each other every now and then, no matter how much we loved each other. I chose to take an afternoon off myself every week, but I usually did something far more sensible than play cards: I went shopping with my best friend, Rebecca Davis. She was an attorney in Jasper Fork, and she could usually get free long enough to join me for an hour or two.

But that was all beside the point. As I was saying, I was supposed to be doing inventory in our walk-in freezer, but I'd gotten lost in a mystery novel one of our customers had left behind, and it was just past eight before I got around to bundling up and heading into our chilly storage area.

The last thing in the world I expected to find when I started poking around in the freezer was a dead body, stiff in more ways than one.

I had absolutely nothing to do with it being there; at least that was what I kept telling Sheriff Croft, though it was pretty clear from the start that he didn't entirely believe me.

Maybe I should back up a little and start from the beginning.

The day before the murder, at just a little past three in the afternoon, we were in the beginnings of that common lull between lunch and dinner that always came as a welcome break. As usual, Mom had worked the grill for the breakfast shift, but she'd gone home when Greg took over the kitchen at eleven. Our first-shift waitress, a single mother named Ellen Hightower, had just finished her workday at two so she could be home and ready when her kids got off the school bus, and our other server, college student Jenny Hollister, wasn't due in until four. We always managed for those two hours, with me covering the tables and also darting to the register whenever I needed to ring up a customer's bill. I had the oddest schedule of all, working the register from six to eight am six days a week, then taking a break until eleven, when I worked until four. I took one more hour off before I came back at five to work until we closed at seven. It made for a long day, but the breaks were nice, and I'd long grown accustomed to the hours, practically growing up in The Charming Moose.

"Order up," Greg said as he rang the small bell in the kitchen to let us know when meals were ready. I smiled at my husband, and he winked as he returned my grin. Greg was a big man, with a firm jaw and a full head of brown hair, and he was every bit as handsome to me now as he was when we'd met twenty years ago during our first year of high school. I'd added a good fifteen pounds since then, but Greg said he liked me that way, and I wasn't crazy enough to try to tell him that he was wrong. He had been the only guy in the entire school who'd played on all of the varsity boys' teams and taken home economics at the same time. Trust me, nobody made fun of his choice of classes back then, and they didn't say a word to him about his cooking now. I was a decent cook myself, but I lacked Greg's skill and imagination. He could take the most common fare—comfort food, really—and turn it into something really special.

As I grabbed the order from the pass-through between the kitchen and the dining room, I glanced at the plate, laden with homemade meatloaf lightly covered with Greg's special tomato sauce, mashed potatoes dotted with tiny dabs of butter, and fresh crisp green beans. There was a substantial dinner roll to go along with it all, and my stomach grumbled at the sight of all of that largesse. As soon as I served Chester Longfield, I was going to have my husband make me up an order just like it.

"Here you go, Chester," I said as I slid the plate in front of him. We had a long gray Formica counter and red vinyl-topped stools that nearly ran all the way across the front of the place, but there were also four booths and eight tables for folks who preferred seating that didn't swivel; Chester had taken up residency at one of those. "Can I top off that sweet tea of yours while I'm here?" I asked.

"You know that I'd be hurt if you didn't," Chester said with a glimmer in his eye. He'd been coming to the diner for nearly fifty years—ever since my grandfather, Moose, had first opened the place at the tender young age of nineteen—and Chester was one of our sea of regulars, an odd array of folks who came by frequently to have a meal with us.

After Chester was taken care of, I grabbed my pad and jotted my own late lunch order down on it. As soon as I hung it on the small spinning rack, Greg's hand reached up and made it disappear.

"That's funny. I didn't hear the front door open," Greg said as he poked his head out through the opening. "Don't tell me Chester wants a repeat."

"That one's for me," I admitted. "It looked so good that I just had to have one myself."

"You know what? I'll make two, and we can try to eat together, just as a change of pace." Given the nature of our business, there was no guarantee that the plan would work, but it was sweet of him to try to share a bite with me.

"It's a date," I said.

While I was waiting for my own meal, I started wiping down the long counter. As I did, a slick-looking tall man in his fifties wearing a fancy suit and carrying an expensive leather briefcase came into the diner.

"Good afternoon. My name is Howard Lance, and I need to speak with the owner of this establishment immediately," he said, and then paused as he glanced at a piece of paper in his hand and asked, "Is this right? Is his name really Moose?" I wasn't thrilled with the man's condescending tone of voice, or the mocking edge buried just beneath it as he said my grandfather's name.

It was time to take him down a notch or two. I pointed to the spot by the cash register where my favorite thing from my childhood sat, a carved wooden moose my grandfather had made for me long ago. He'd crafted it out of walnut, and the lush patina of the wood had grown richer and richer over the years.

"Direct your comments and complaints straight to him," I said as I pointed with my ballpoint pen in the carved animal's direction. "He doesn't mind listening one bit, but don't expect much of a reply. Moose is what you might call a little reserved when he's around strangers."

The man looked clearly flustered by my comment as he glanced at my wooden moose. "I'm sorry, but I must not have made myself clear. I need to speak with the diner's owner," he repeated.

Greg came out from the kitchen wearing his apron, where he usually spent his days creating our lunch and dinner offerings, making everything himself from scratch, from apple pie to fried zucchini. His natural expression almost always included a smile, but at the moment, there was a storm brewing in his eyes. "Is there a problem, Victoria?"

"This man's looking to have a word with Moose, but when I pointed him out, he got kind of quiet."

Greg nodded knowingly. "It doesn't surprise me. Moose is like that sometimes."

"That's what I told him."

The man looked at each of us in turn as though we'd lost our minds. "What kind of loony bin have I walked into?"

"Lower your voice, or you'll hurt Moose's feelings," I said. "He may look tough on the outside, but he's got a truly sensitive soul." Moose had been with me since kindergarten, and when I'd taken over the family restaurant, the first thing I'd done was to make sure there was a place for him right up front beside me.

"For a place named Charming, nobody is being very pleasant with me," the man said.

My dad had always disliked the name The Charming Moose, and he'd tried to turn the place into Joe's the second he took over, but no one in Jasper Fork would stand for it, and he soon gave up and learned to accept it. As for me, I liked the name. I thought it gave the place some character, and more than a little style.

"Mr. Lance, you have to be cordial to get it back in return," I said.

The frustration was clearly growing in his voice as he said, "Whatever. I've had about all the nonsense I'm going to take. Now, I'm asking you people for the last time, who's in charge here?"

He'd directed his question to Greg, another big mistake on his part.

My husband shook his head as he replied, "Don't look at

me. You'll have to talk to the lady. She's the boss."

"This isn't your business?" he asked as he looked directly at my husband.

"Me? No way. I may be the chief cook and bottle washer around here, but Victoria's the one who runs the diner. If you have something to say, you're going to need to take it up with her. Now if you'll excuse me, I've got an apple pie in the oven that's nearly ready to come out."

I watched Greg duck back into the kitchen. No doubt he thought that he'd be safe there from my wrath over the fallout of this particular conversation, but I wasn't so sure. I was getting tired of tap-dancing with this guy. "What exactly can I do for you, Mr. Lance?"

He opened his briefcase and slapped a document down on the counter in front of me. "You can give this to Moose Nelson the next time you see him, and tell him that he has ten days to respond to this, or suffer the consequences. Good day."

Before he could leave, I said, "I don't know. I think it's a little windy out."

He turned and looked at me again. "What are you talking about?"

"You said that it was a good day, and I commented on the weather from my own perspective. The middle of October can be a bit blustery for my taste. What part of that conversation didn't you understand?"

He didn't even try to come up with a response as he stormed out of the diner.

After he was gone, I glanced at the paper he'd left.

I was about to crumple it up and toss it in the trash when something pretty dire shouted out from the heading, so I started reading it more carefully.

Greg came out a few minutes later with two full plates of our meatloaf special.

I glanced up at him and said worriedly, "Thanks, but I've suddenly lost my appetite."

He looked down at the plates and frowned. "I could

always make you something else, if this doesn't sound good anymore."

"It's not the food. It's this."

Greg put the plates down on the counter and took the document from me. He scanned it, and then shook his head in disbelief. We weren't doing his food any justice letting it cool like that, but there was just no helping it. My husband said, "Victoria, this is serious. We need to find your grandfather, and fast."

"He's still fishing at Cloud Lake with my dad," I said. Father and son took a week off alone every year to go fishing, staying at a cabin that my grandfather had built himself on the mountain lake. There was no electricity or running water at the cabin, but neither man seemed to mind the lack of modern amenities. Moose spent quite a bit of time up there by himself, but my grandmother, Martha, didn't seem to mind his absences. She claimed she was happy for the time away from him, but it was clear they still loved each other very much. They'd both retired from running the diner eight years before, and my father had grown weary of the grind after only a few years of being in charge. He'd moved on to other jobs, though Mom had stayed on when Greg and I had taken over.

I went on, "You know there's no cell phone coverage up there, so the only way we're going to talk with either one of them is to drive up to the lake ourselves, and we don't have time to do that, not if we're going to keep the diner open today."

"I'd be happy to go for you," Chester volunteered from his seat not far away. To be honest, I'd forgotten he was still there.

"It's sweet of you to offer, but do you even know where the cabin is?" I asked.

Chester laughed. "I've spent more than one night with Moose at the lake. I could find it in the dark, which I'll have to do, if I don't get going pretty soon. I hate this time change. It always throws off my system."

"Thanks for offering, but we'll figure something out," I said hastily.

Chester wouldn't hear of it, though. "Nonsense, my seventeen-year-old grandson has been clamoring for some quality time with me for months—only the stars above know why—so I'll let him drive me. Trust me, it will be our pleasure."

"Are you sure?" I asked.

"We really don't have much choice, Victoria," Greg said. He turned to Chester and said, "We'd be in your debt."

"Believe me, the pleasure is mine."

Chester reached for his wallet, but I plucked his bill out of his hand and tore it into two pieces. "Your money's no good here today, sir."

He looked quite pleased by the prospect. "In that case, I'll take some of that apple pie that smells so heavenly with me for the trip."

He'd clearly been kidding, but Greg retrieved the pie he'd made earlier and boxed up two large slabs of it up. "For you and your grandson," Greg said.

As he presented the box to Chester, the older man said, "That's not necessary. I was just teasing you."

"It's the least we can do. Enjoy it."

"I will," he said as he started for the door. Chester paused, and then he turned back to me. "What exactly is it that I'm supposed to tell him, Victoria? Moose might not be ready to leave, and I don't need to tell you how stubborn your grandfather can be at times."

"Just tell him that Rome is burning," I said simply.

"That's it?"

"Believe me, it will be enough."

After Chester was gone, Greg asked, "Shouldn't you have given him more information than that? It was kind of cryptic, wasn't it?"

"More information would only complicate things. There's been a longstanding family tradition that in dire times, that phrase will bring every able body running, no questions asked."

Greg looked a little hurt, so I asked him, "What's wrong?"

"Why haven't I heard about this before now? After all, I've been married to you for twelve years. Doesn't that make me a member of your family, too?"

"Of course it does." I wrapped my arms around my husband as I explained, "The only reason you haven't heard it is because we haven't had a major crisis in all this time." After giving him a reassuring hug and a quick peck, I added, "There's nothing we can do about this until Moose gets here. Why don't we go ahead and eat?"

Greg looked down at the plates, and then said, "Forget it. Everything's cold now."

"I'm sure it will be fine," I said as I grabbed a fork.

He wouldn't hear of it, though. "Let me at least warm these up. I'll be right back."

I wasn't about to argue, and after he took the plates back into the kitchen, I looked at the document one more time.

It appeared to be official enough, but I couldn't testify about the validity of the claim.

One thing was certain.

EVICTION NOTICE and REPOSSESSION were printed in large enough letters to get anyone's attention.

I just hoped my grandfather could clear it up, or The Charming Moose was going to be in some serious trouble, and soon.

I picked up the phone to call Rebecca, but I stopped mid-dial and put it back in the cradle. I'd almost forgotten that my best friend was out of town at a legal conference at the moment, and as much as I wanted her official opinion about this document, I wasn't about to disturb her unless it turned out to be absolutely necessary.

It was twenty minutes until our normal closing time at seven, and there was still no sign of my grandfather. I hoped that Chester and his grandson hadn't had any trouble on their way to the lake. If anything had happened to them while they'd been doing something for me, I wasn't sure I'd ever be able to forgive myself.

Greg kept poking his head out of the pass-through to scan the dining room.

"Would you stop doing that?" I asked. "You're making me nervous, and Jenny nearly dropped a bowl of mac and cheese a few minutes ago."

"I did not," our youngest server said with a laugh as she came by to pick up a bowl of Greg's homemade chicken soup and a grilled cheese sandwich for Counter Seat 12. Jenny was a college student, and a godsend for us, happy to work a three-hour shift every afternoon and evening that wasn't enough for most folks looking for a job. "And you're as bad as he is, Victoria. Who exactly is it that we're all waiting for?"

"Moose is coming back home tonight," I said.

"That's the best news I've heard all day." For some odd reason, Jenny seemed to gravitate toward my grandfather, and it was pretty clear that he didn't mind the attention of the pretty young blonde.

"I just wish it were for a better reason," Greg said as he ducked his head back into the kitchen.

Just as my husband disappeared, the front door slammed open and my grandfather rushed in. His gray hair was unkempt, and there was a six-day stubble of beard on his face, but his eyes were still clear, his back arrow-straight, and his demeanor commanding.

"Where's the fire?" he bellowed.

That got the immediate attention of our final two diners. Hastily, I told them, "There's no fire, folks. Everything is fine. It's just an expression."

That seemed to soothe their nerves, but Moose looked confused. "Chester told me that Rome was burning."

I nodded. "It is, but would you mind lowering your voice? Or do you honestly want all of Jasper Fork knowing our business?"

That calmed my grandfather down in a hurry. Running the diner for all those years, Moose had heard more from the kitchen about the secret goings on and behind-the-scenes events in our small community than anyone else in town, and he knew full well how fast rumors could spread. "You're right. Let's continue this in back."

Jenny protested, "But that's not fair. I won't be able to hear what's going on if you both move back there."

Moose patted her hand. "Don't worry, child. I'm sure my granddaughter will bring you up to speed soon enough."

Moose followed me into the kitchen, where we'd kept the notice since Mr. Lance had first delivered it.

"Where's Dad?" I asked him.

"He went to get your mother and grandmother. It sounded as though we needed to have a family meeting, and they're all a part of this crazed clan just as much as your husband standing over there is."

Greg nodded, and I was sure that he appreciated being included, even in times of turmoil. He had come from a broken home, and when he'd married me, he'd found a sense of belonging that he'd missed so dearly as a kid.

"Should we wait for them?" I asked.

"I don't want to, but then again, I don't figure we have much choice." He looked over at Greg. "Any chance I could get a bit of that chili of yours while we're waiting?"

"You bet," he said. Greg scooped out a huge portion and added a large chunk of cheddar and a hunk of cornbread to the heaping bowl. This was no ordinary fare. Rich chunks of stew beef were seasoned with onion, garlic, chili powder, and handful of other spices I recognized. A bowl of my husband's chili was a legitimate meal in and of itself. Greg's cornbread was a little sweeter than most, but it was the perfect complement to the spices in the chili.

Moose took a seat by the prep counter and promptly devoured it all, asking only for a refill of the chilled milk I'd given him a few moments before.

"I'd deny it under oath in open court if you ever repeated

it," my grandfather said as he quickly scraped the bottom of his bowl, "but I like your chili better than what I make, and that's saying something."

"That's funny, I like yours better, myself," Greg said.

Both men smiled, and I could feel the warmth and affection pass between them. My dad had lacked what it took to run the diner, and no one had been more aware of it than my grandfather, but in Greg—and in me—Moose had found true kindred spirits to carry on his legacy.

As he pushed his bowl away, the kitchen door flew open and my parents hurried in, along with my grandmother. While Moose's face was grizzled, my dad's cheeks were bare.

"You stopped to shave, even after you heard that Rome was burning?" I asked, not believing my own eyes.

Moose laughed. "Not even Joe is that crazy. Your dad took an electric razor with him to the cabin."

"There's no shame in trying to always look presentable," my father said. He had some of Moose's genes in him, but whereas my grandfather was robust and open, my dad was quite a bit more reserved. I wondered how hard it must have been for him growing up in his father's long shadow, and at that moment, I started to understand my father just a little bit better than I ever had before.

"Come here and give me a kiss, you old man," my grandmother said to her husband. "I know it's hard to imagine, but I actually missed you."

"Like this? I'm a tad unkempt."

"I don't care what state you're in."

She kissed him soundly, and then Moose said, "We're all here now, Victoria. What seems to be the emergency?"

"It's this," I said as I handed him the document Howard Lance had delivered earlier that day.

"Eviction," he said as he read the top line. "That's complete and utter nonsense."

"I'm not so sure it is," Greg said. "It looks official enough to me."

"I bought the land this diner stands on myself from Joshua Lance fifty years ago."

My face must have whitened because my grandfather asked, "What's wrong? What did I say?"

"Lance. The man who delivered this paper today said his name was Howard Lance."

"How old was he?"

"Mid-fifties, I'd say."

That brought a frown to Moose's face. "I suppose he could be Joshua's boy, but I can't be sure. All I know is that Joshua Lance sold me this land just before he moved to Hickory, and I haven't heard a word from him since. At the time, he had to have owned ten percent of Jasper Fork when he started selling it off at rock-bottom prices. Quite a few of us bought land from him."

My dad spoke up. "Did any of you have your titles searched at the courthouse when you made the purchases?"

Moose shrugged. "I don't believe so. As I remember it, it was just a cash-and-handshake deal."

My father looked exasperated. "Did you at least have the transfer of ownership registered at the clerk's office?"

Moose looked angrily at my dad. "How could I possibly remember that from all those years ago? I've lived a full life since then, boy."

Martha touched her husband's shoulder. "Calm down, Moose. Joseph is just trying to help us determine if we should be concerned about this." Nobody in the world called my father Joseph except my grandmother. I still called my parents Mom and Dad, but Moose and Martha had always insisted on being called just that, even when I'd been a toddler. Neither one of them had cared for the grandfather/grandmother monikers.

"I'm perfectly calm," Moose said dismissively. He tapped the document with his index finger as he added, "Something's got to be done about this."

"I know a lawyer in Lenoir we could get to look into the legality of this," my father said.

"We could always call Rebecca," I chimed in. I was having second thoughts about not interrupting her conference. This was, in a very real way, life and death for me and my family.

"Joe, Victoria, there's no offense intended, but I aim to take this to the top," Moose said gravely.

"Are you going to call the governor?" Greg asked. Rumor was that the state's highest elected official and Moose went way back, but I'd never been able to discover if it were true, or if Moose had just started the rumor himself for his own entertainment.

My grandfather shook his head. "No, I'm going to need somebody higher in authority than that. I'm calling Holly Dixon."

My grandmother immediately bristled beside him. "There's no need to do that, and you know it."

He took her hands in his. "Martha, I told you a long time ago, there was never anything between Holly and me but simple conversation. We need her now, and there's no reason not to call her."

"I saw what I saw, and I know what I know," my grandmother said.

"Hang on a second," Greg said. "Are we talking about Judge Dixon?"

"Who else could we be discussing?" Moose asked. "She was Holly to me before she ever dreamed about becoming a judge."

"She dreamed about being Mrs. Moose Nelson before she ever thought about going to law school," my grandmother said sharply. Clearly, she was actually jealous of the woman, even after all of these years.

"Then I won't call her," Moose said with a sigh. "We'll manage to get through this without her. I didn't disrespect you then, and I won't do it now, Martha."

My grandmother looked at him a few moments, and then she took his face in her hands and planted a solid kiss on his lips.

"What was that for?" he asked her.

"For the gesture, and the sentiment. Now, go ahead and call her."

Moose looked at her as though she'd just started speaking French. "Say again?"

"Call Judge Tart. If she can help us, I'm not above asking for it."

"Go on," I said, "Call her before Martha changes her mind."

He glanced at the portable telephone I was shoving toward him as though it were radioactive, but he refused to take it. "Let's all just take a deep breath and think about this for a minute."

"We don't have time," I said. "If we lose this place, we all know that a part of our family's going to die with it."

"You're right," Moose said. "Somebody give me a phone book."

Instead of answering his request, Martha kissed him once again.

"I'm not even going to pretend to know what that one was for," Moose said.

Martha started to tell him when she saw me smiling. "Ask Victoria. She knows."

I grinned. "I'm guessing it's because you have to look her number up."

"Why wouldn't I?" he asked, still clearly perplexed.

"That's the point. You wouldn't, if you knew it by heart," I said.

Moose just shook his head. "I swear, trying to figure out women is a waste of a man's time and brainpower."

My mother, Melinda, who had been quiet up until now, said with the hint of a smile, "And we all know that you don't have that much of either one to spare at the moment." She was where I'd gotten my sassy streak, though she didn't show it all that much anymore.

Greg laughed as he commented, "Take my word for it and give up while you're still just a little behind, Moose."

"That's a fair piece of advice, and I aim to take it," Moose said as he looked up the judge's number in our local phone book. I may not have had any reason to have hope, but I was beginning to believe that we might just have a chance to save the diner after all. It wasn't necessarily because of anything that anyone had said, or the plans we were making.

It was because my family was working on the problem together, and that gave me more encouragement than I could describe.

At least that was how I felt until Judge Dixon showed up fifteen minutes later.

Chapter 2

Martha excused herself as Moose made the call to Judge Dixon, and no one was really all that surprised when she left the diner altogether soon afterward, especially not my grandfather. We had just two customers at the moment, so I took the opportunity to hang the CLOSED sign on the front door and sent Jenny on her way, though it was still a bit early. My two regulars were soon gone, so I stayed by the door to let Judge Dixon in when she showed up. When the judge finally appeared at The Charming Moose, I let her in, and as she stepped inside, she scanned the dining room quickly. I had to wonder if she was searching for my grandmother.

I smiled at her and said, "Don't worry. She's not here."

"She?" the judge asked archly, making one word sound more like an accusation than a simple query. In her late-sixties, the woman was stern and direct, and she wore her gray hair pulled back into a bun so tight it was amazing that she didn't smile more often just from the pressure alone, but I could see that deep down, she was still quite a lovely woman.

"My grandmother had to leave," I said, "but everyone else is in the kitchen. Would you care to join us there?"

Judge Dixon waved a shooing hand in the air, gesturing for me to lead on. I didn't really have a response to that, and besides, she scared me more than a little bit with her judicial air that didn't need a robe to back it up.

As we walked into the kitchen, I saw Moose's face soften for just an instant, and I turned to catch a matching glimpse of the judge's demeanor just before she carefully masked it again. It was clear that, regardless of the circumstances, she was happy to see my grandfather, even if most of his family was surrounding him at the moment.

Getting her composure back, she said, "First things first,

Moose. Let's see that document."

My grandfather offered it to her as he said, "Thanks for coming, Holly."

"Of course," she answered. The judge studied the document carefully, and then after a few moments of consideration, she said, "I'm afraid it's all in order, as far as it goes. This notice appears to be legal and binding."

"But I bought this land fifty years ago!" Moose protested. "I paid good money for it."

If his abrupt tone bothered her in the least, she didn't show it. "Do you happen to have the original bill of sale?"

Moose just shrugged. "Honestly, if I ever did have one, it's probably long gone by now. We did business a little differently back then."

"How about the diner's safety deposit box?" my father asked. "Could you have stored it there and forgotten about it, Moose? When I had to check it once, it was jam full of all kinds of papers."

"I might have stuck it there, but then again, there's just as much a chance that I used the back of it to write a takeout order down two days later."

"I believe that it would be prudent on your part to find it," Judge Dixon said. As she tapped the paper, she added, "This document could present you with a great deal of trouble."

"All I can do is look for it," Moose said. "Can you suggest anything else we might be able to do to make this mess go away?"

"If I were you, I'd try the courthouse in the morning. If the sale and property transfer were properly registered there, you should be able to win a court case if it comes to that." She added, almost as an afterthought, "I'd have to recuse myself from the case, of course."

"Of course," Moose said. "While you're here, can I get you a slice of pie? You used to like cherry, if I remember correctly."

I know it wasn't my imagination that time. She softened,

but just around the edges, and only for a moment. "I'm afraid there's no time, but thank you for your kind offer."

After she was gone, I asked Moose, "What exactly was that all about?"

"What are you talking about?"

"Come on, I saw it, and so did everyone else here. Something happened way back then between the two of you, didn't it? I'm willing to bet that it was more than just casual conversation, too."

"Child, you're delusional," Moose said.

"But you didn't say that she was wrong," my mother chimed in.

Moose looked as though he wanted to say something, and then he obviously thought better of it. He rubbed his chin whiskers and then he declared, "I need a shower, a shave, and a good night's sleep. We'll deal with this in the morning." As he headed for the door, he turned to his son and daughter-in-law. "Are you two driving me home, or do I have to walk?"

Once they were gone, I looked at Greg, and found that he was smiling at me. "What's so amusing?"

"I don't know a single other person in all of Jasper Fork with the courage to tackle your grandfather head-on like you just did, and yet you did it without any sense of concern for your safety or wellbeing. Remind me never to cross you, Victoria."

"I don't know what you're talking about," I said with a smile. "I just asked the man a simple question."

"Whatever you say." Greg looked at the clock. "Let's clean up and get out of here. I'm tired, and I have a feeling tomorrow is going to be a long day. I'm going to cancel the poker game tomorrow night."

"Don't you dare," I said. "You need your time away from this place, and besides, what are you going to be able to do to help our cause at night? As a matter of fact, it couldn't hurt for you to show up and see what your poker buddies have to say. That's one of the most influential groups in town, and if we can get them on our side, it couldn't hurt."

"You've convinced me," he said with the hint of a smile. "I'm going after all."

As we went about our nightly routine of closing, I balanced the cash register and swept the front while Greg took care of cleaning up the kitchen. The dining room was in good shape when my husband came out to join me, and as we headed home, I couldn't help wondering if tonight was the beginning of the end for our comfortable and safe little world.

"Come on, open up," Greg said the next morning as he knocked again and again on the front door. We were waiting on the courthouse steps, it was two minutes until nine, and my husband and I were there to see if any official records of the land sale between Moose and Joshua Lance existed. At the same time we were waiting to check the books, Moose and Martha were going to be visiting the bank, hoping to find the original receipt tucked away in the diner's safety deposit box. While we were all chasing down leads, Mom was running the grill, and Dad had even taken a little time off from his job to help out up front.

"You know, they aren't going to open early just because you want them to," I said to my husband with a half-smile.

"Why couldn't Judge Dixon have taken care of this last night?" Greg asked. "She has to have some kind of pull here."

I tugged my jacket closer, wishing I'd worn a heavier coat when I'd left the house. We were close enough to the mountains to get their weather sometimes, and this autumn was turning out to be chillier than most. I loved the explosion of colors the hardwood trees brought with the season, so I was willing to deal with whatever weather we faced, but that didn't mean I had to embrace it. On the other hand, my husband didn't even seem to notice the change in temperature.

"Greg, aren't you cold?"

"It's a little brisk," he admitted as he looked around, "but that's the way I like it."

Somehow, seeing him in just a T-shirt and blue jeans made me even colder.

Hank Brewer didn't even seem to notice us as he approached the courthouse, a scowl plastered to his face. Hank was a tall and heavyset man with a shock of white hair. He was a longtime friend of Moose's, and owned The Clothes Horse just down the block from us.

"What are you two doing here?" he asked when he finally saw us. Before I could answer, he did it for me. As his expression soured even further, he said, "Don't tell me. You got a visit from Howard Lance yesterday, too, didn't you? Does Moose know about this mess yet?"

"He found out last night," I said.

"Then I'm surprised that Howard Lance is still walking around today. I'm tempted to take a swing at him myself, but Moose must want to kill him."

Behind him, another citizen of Jasper Fork, Cynthia Wilson, came up and joined us. I'd gone to school with Cynthia's daughter, Penny. She must have heard our topic of conversation as she approached. "I didn't sleep a wink last night. I've been so worried about this entire mess." Cynthia ran A Cut Above, the town beauty parlor. "I've been trying to figure out what to do, but I'm not afraid to admit that I'm in way over my head. I don't know what I'll do if he takes away my business."

"This is all just unbelievable. Moose isn't even sure that he kept his receipt for the original land sale," I said.

"I lost my papers in a basement flood ten years ago," Hank said. "But I know for a fact I registered the sale, so I should be okay."

"I spoke with my mother in Florida, and she's certain that she registered too, not that she's still not as frantic as I am." That didn't surprise me one bit. Evelyn, and her daughter as well, had an overactive imagination when it came to bad

things happening to her, and there wasn't a conclusion yet
that either one of them hadn't jumped to as far as I knew.

"How is Evelyn doing?" Hank asked her.

"You know her. She never changes," Cynthia said with a
smile.

"Give her my love the next time you talk to her. I'm
guessing you two will be chatting later today."

"No doubt about it," Cynthia said. "I'm supposed to call
her just as soon as I have Karen make a copy of the record in
the Book of Deeds and shove it under Howard Lance's
nose."

"Funny, I've been considering putting it somewhere else,
myself," Hank said.

Karen Morgan, our official town clerk, came out at nine
o'clock, adjusting the beehive hairdo she'd preferred ever
since I'd known her. The woman never seemed to age, and if
that was the price for a lifetime beehive, I might consider it
myself someday. On second thought, even if it was the
fountain of youth, I was probably just going to have to pass.

Immortality just wasn't worth it.

"Goodness, how long have you folks been out here in the
cold? If I'd seen you earlier, I would have let you in."

We all walked in together, and as soon as Karen got
behind the desk, she asked, "Now, who needs to be taken
care of first?"

Before Greg or I could say anything, Hank pointed to us.
"Take them. They were here when I showed up."

Cynthia nodded in agreement, so Karen looked at me
expectantly.

"I need to see if there's a record of Moose's land
purchase from Joshua Lance. I'm sorry, but I don't have the
exact date of the sale."

Hank spoke up. "Moose and Evelyn bought their land
the same day I did. It was March 11, 1959."

"How on earth do you remember that far back?" I asked.

Hank looked sheepish as he admitted, "My daughter was
born that day, and I slipped out of the hospital to pay Joshua

for his land. I didn't think Sally would even notice I was gone, and Joshua said if I didn't show up with my money that day, he was going to sell the property to someone else. I couldn't take the chance, but I've been hearing about it on the eleventh of March ever since. I'm pretty certain I recorded the deed on the way back to the hospital, just in case Joshua got any funny ideas about our deal."

"That's the date for all of us, then," I said.

Karen smiled. "Excellent. That should save me a few hours of work."

She bypassed her computer and headed for the open stacks behind us. They were available to anyone in Jasper Fork who wanted to check any vital records or deeds, since everything was registered in a new set of volumes each year.

As she started digging through the books, Greg asked her, "You're kidding, right? Isn't this all computerized now?"

Karen laughed. "We were told two years ago that someday the old records would be added to our database, but there's never been enough funding to do it. Don't worry, these handwritten notations serve just as well."

As Karen perused the stacks, an unsettled look came across her face. "Now that's odd."

I had a sinking feeling in the pit of my stomach. "What's wrong?"

"I'm sure it's nothing," Karen said as she searched the shelves a little more intently.

"Don't try to snow us, woman; it's clear that something's not right," Hank said.

Karen kept scanning the dusty old volumes, but she finally gave up and said, "I'm sure it's just been misfiled, but the record book for March of 1959 seems to be missing."

"Are you sure you're looking in the right place?" Greg asked as he moved toward the stacks to join her. "No offense, but this place is a wreck."

"Why should I take offense at that?" Karen asked, though it was clear in her voice that she was hurt by the implication.

"I'm just in this room part-time, so there's no way I can watch over everything. You wouldn't believe the amount of responsibilities I have here."

"We all know that you do a marvelous job within a limited amount of time," I said, doing my best to reassure her. "Karen, you have to forgive us. We're so stressed out about the eviction notice we all got that we're snapping at everyone."

"Is that what this is all about? How horrible for all of you."

I looked at Greg, gave him one of my best piercing looks, and he nodded. Turning to Karen, my husband put on his most charming smile. "I hope that you can find it in your heart to forgive me. I didn't mean anything by what I just said. Frankly, I think it's amazing what you manage to do here every day. It must feel like you're constantly herding cats."

Greg had been fine up until the last word, but I knew that he'd gotten himself into even more trouble than he had before when he said it. Karen owned at least three cats that I knew of, and in lieu of children, they were the only family she had.

I saw her neck stiffen, and then she asked him pointedly, "Now, why on earth would anyone want to herd cats? That sounds absolutely barbaric."

"It's just an old expression," I said.

"Well, it's horrid, if you ask me."

It was time to change the subject back to the matter at hand. "Are we sure the book wasn't just misfiled? With so many folks coming in, it would be impossible for something not to get misplaced every now and then."

Karen shrugged, and then pointed to the shelf. There was a distinctly empty gap between 1958 and 1960. I leaned closer to the shelf and studied the empty space between the two books that were still there. Taking out my hanky, I ran it across the bare wood of the gap, and then I looked at it. "One thing's for sure, this book hasn't been gone long," I said as I held my hanky up. It was as pristine as when I'd pulled it out of the dryer the day before. "There's not the slightest trace of dust on this."

"Dust does seem to accumulate down here," Karen admitted.

"Do you have any idea who's been in this room in the past two weeks?" Hank asked. "Is there some kind of register folks have to use?"

"There used to be, but it disappeared, as well," she admitted with a frown.

"When did that happen?" I asked.

"Two weeks ago," Karen admitted. "I asked Lynette upstairs to order me a new one, but she never got around to it. I wouldn't do you much good anyway, since we operate on the honor system around here. I doubt a thief would steal it when it would be easier just not to sign it in the first place."

"Unless they weren't planning the theft when they first came in here," I said. "The ledger could have been stolen to cover their tracks."

"I don't believe this!" Cynthia said. "What am I going to tell my mother?"

"Tell her not to panic, and that we're digging into this," I said.

"Is your grandfather going to work on it, too?" Cynthia asked. "My mom always did like Moose."

"She most likely had to get in line," Greg said. "Apparently the man's had his fair share of admirers over the years in Jasper Fork."

Cynthia looked at him oddly. "What exactly is that supposed to mean?"

"He just seems to have an affinity for the women in Jasper Fork," Greg answered. "You have to admit, the man can be a real charmer."

"There's no doubt about that," Cynthia reluctantly agreed. "I'll let Mom know what's going on, and I hope you will keep me in the loop about what you find."

"We'll add you to the list," I said. My husband's

unbridled candor was one reason that I was happy he worked in the kitchen and not directly with the customers at our diner.

Hank said, "I wouldn't mind getting a call, myself. I'm sure I'll talk to Moose later. For more reasons than I can name, I wish Helen were still alive. She'd know exactly what to do. My wife has been gone three years, and I still reach across the bed to kiss her good night just before I go to sleep."

"Try not to worry. We'll be in touch," I said as Hank and Cynthia left.

"Well, what do we do now?" I asked Greg.

He rubbed his hands together. "We've got over an hour before we have to take over at the diner. I suggest we keep looking for that missing book. After all, we might just be panicking about nothing. It wouldn't be hard for someone to put it back in the wrong, would it?"

"I suppose it's possible," I said, but the missing record of deeds combined with the AWOL logbook gave me a hunch that we were wasting our time.

Unfortunately, an hour later, I knew that my instincts had been right all along. We hadn't been able to come up with anything new.

I just hoped that Moose and Martha had better luck than we had.

Unfortunately, we soon found out that they hadn't fared any better themselves.

After thoroughly checking the safety deposit box, they discovered that there was no receipt. It appeared that my grandfather had no record of ever having owned the land and that our diner, our family's source of income and the place we called home during working hours, might not belong to us after all.

Greg's Homemade Chili

This has been one of my family's standard meals for many years. We love this any time of year! It's especially good when the snow outside is flying, and the wind is howling through the trees. There's just something about this meal that makes me feel safe, and happy to have those I love around me.

Ingredients

1 pound ground beef, 80/20
1 medium onion, diced, yellow or white
1 clove, garlic, minced (optional)
1 15 oz. (approximate) can tomato sauce
3 Tablespoons chili powder
1 teaspoon salt
1 teaspoon black pepper
1 teaspoon sugar
2 teaspoons Worcestershire sauce
1 15 oz. (approximate) can dark red kidney beans, drained

Directions

In a large pan, cook the ground beef, diced onion, (and garlic, if preferred) until the ground beef is light brown. Drain the beef, then add the tomato sauce, chili powder, sugar, salt, pepper, and Worcestershire sauce. Stir all together, and then bring to a boil. Back off to a simmer, cover, and cook for one hour, stirring occasionally. Add the drained kidney beans, stir them in, and then heat for 15-20 minutes. Serve with sour cream if desired, and top with cheddar cheese.

Chapter 3

"Order up," Greg said as he hit the bell once a little while after we started our shifts together at eleven. I glanced at the plate, and then grabbed it to deliver myself before Ellen got it.

"Thanks," she said as we passed each other. She had a pot of coffee and was refilling our early lunch diners' mugs, and I liked to help out whenever I could if the register wasn't busy.

I took the plate of country fried steak, onion wedges, and French fries, and put them down in front of Reverend Mercer.

"Here's your meal," I said as I smiled at him. "When is your wife getting back into town?"

"How did you know that she was even gone?" he asked as he returned my smile. He was a portly older man with quick blue eyes and a ready smile, but he wasn't usually a regular at the diner.

"Do you mean besides the fact that you usually don't come by for lunch, or the fact that you're ordering off the menu like a man temporarily off his leash?"

He held both hands up in the air, his smile never wavering. "You caught me. Miriam is out of town visiting with her niece, and I had to stay behind to deliver Jackson Briggs' eulogy."

At least there had been no suspicion surrounding that passing. Jackson had been ninety-three years old, and he'd simply faded away in his sleep a few nights before.

"How's Dagmar holding up?" Dagmar was Jackson's wife of seventy years, though he'd called her his bride until the day that he died.

"Truthfully, she accepted it a long time ago. When Jackson was sixty, his doctor gave him six months to live.

Jackson outlived the man by over thirty years, so he always felt as though he was living on borrowed time, and he was going to make the most of it."

"Are any of the kids in town for the funeral?" I asked.

"Oh yes. There are children, grandchildren, and great-grandchildren running all around that house. I offered to put some up myself, but Dagmar insisted that she loved the company. The service is going to be more of a celebration than a somber occasion, and I'm having a little difficulty reaching the exact tone that Dagmar expects."

She was a woman of strong opinions, and I knew that Reverend Mercer didn't want to let her down.

"Why don't you treat it like a retirement party instead of a funeral?" I suggested. "After all, isn't that exactly what it is, in a way?"

The reverend looked troubled by the suggestion. "Do you mean that we should have balloons and cake at the service instead of flowers?"

"No, of course not. At least not unless Dagmar approves of it. I'm talking about showing pictures, maybe even slides, recapping the highlights of Jackson's life. Folks could tell stories about him, if they'd like. The man was quite the character, so you shouldn't have any shortage of volunteers for tales about his past."

The reverend considered it for a moment, and then nodded. "I believe that's exactly what she is hoping for. I'll run it by Dagmar."

As he started to get up, I asked, "Wouldn't it be okay for you to eat first? I'd hate to see this food just go to waste."

"That makes two of us," he said as he sat back down. "Thank you for the idea. I'll be sure that you get full credit."

"Please don't," I said. "There's no reason anyone has to know that we brainstormed this together. Let's just hope that it satisfies the family."

"The family will be happy if Dagmar is," he said as he took his first bite. A true smile spread across his face. "That is magic. Please give my compliments to the chef."

"I'd be happy to," I said as I topped off his iced tea.

I returned to the pass-through window and told Greg, "The reverend passes on his compliments for your cooking."

"I knew there was a reason I liked that man," Greg said. "Has Moose checked in yet?"

"No, but evidently there are quite a few folks around town who did business with Joshua Lance, and Moose is determined to talk to every last one of them."

"What's he hoping to find?" I asked.

"Anything that might help," Greg said. He pointed behind me as he said, "The Harpers look like they're ready to pay their bill."

"I'm on it," I said as I hurried over to the register.

The day seemed to drag by. At five, Greg came out carrying two platters of his pulled-pork barbeque sandwiches, along with enough French fries to cover the balance of the plates.

"What's this about?" I asked.

"We both have to eat, and we've got a break right now. Things are kind of slow at the moment, something that usually doesn't happen this time of day."

"What about Jenny?" I asked.

"She can eat after we do, and you can wait on customers and ring them up. Come on, we might not have much time."

I did as he asked, and as soon as the first bite of sandwich hit my mouth, I was glad that he had. The South was known for its barbeque, and while a great many folks admired the Lexington style of barbeque, I preferred my husband's. To my amazement, we had nearly thirty minutes before Greg had to cook the next order. Those times were magical to me, and I treasured every one of them.

As it approached six, Moose still wasn't back at the diner.

Greg poked his head out the pass-through window and said, "I know what you said before, and you made a convincing argument, but I'm going to call the guys and get out of this week's poker game after all," Greg said as he put his spatula aside and reached for the phone.

"Don't do that," I said.

"Why not? I can't see taking off to have fun while we've all got this hanging over our heads. The more I think about it, the less I'm willing to do it."

"Greg, I appreciate the sentiment, but how's it going to look if you don't show up? We don't have anything to hide, and I have faith that it's going to work out. Besides, if this goes to court, who better to have behind us than your poker buddies? The mayor might be able to help our cause, and the sheriff as well."

"Tell you what. If Moose shows up in the next ten minutes, I'll go. If not, I'm hanging around here, no matter what. Agreed?"

I was about to answer when the front door opened, and Moose walked in with my mother at his side. Dad and my grandmother were nowhere to be seen, and it had to make me wonder if my grandfather had had any luck polling his friends.

"In the kitchen," he gestured to me abruptly as he blew past me.

Before I ducked in to join them, I told Jenny, "Get the register, would you? This shouldn't take long."

"You know me. I'm always glad to help out," she said, and I followed everyone else into the back.

"Did you have any luck with any of the rest of them?" I asked Moose as soon as I was back with them.

"I spoke with eleven people besides the ones we've already talked to," my grandfather said. "Joshua was a busy man that day he sold off his property. Nine of them had receipts, so they should be fine."

"How about the other two?" Greg asked.

"Bob Chastain swears that up until recently, he had a receipt for the land his auto repair shop is on. He claims it was framed and mounted on his office wall, but when we both looked for it, it was gone. Francie Humphries had already been served as well, and she was beside herself with worry. She makes Cynthia Wilson look calm and rational, if that gives you any idea how she's taking it."

"Hang on a second," I said. "How did Howard Lance know exactly who to serve papers to in the first place?"

"That's the same thing that I started wondering, but it turns out that it wasn't all that hard. He just hit everyone his old man did business with that day," Moose said with a slight smile.

"What's so good about that?" Greg asked.

"It proves that he didn't know who still had receipts, and who didn't," I said. "If he stole the 1959 record book, he knew who Joshua did business with, but he couldn't be sure that everyone didn't still have their receipts for the original transactions. Old Howard must have decided to shotgun out the paperwork and see if he got any hits."

"Then that proves that he's a crook," Greg said with an answering grin. "All a judge has to do is look at that to know that he doesn't have a case against any of us."

"Not so much," Moose said. "I ran it by Holly, and she says that it might not matter. She has a hunch that these are nuisance suits and nothing else, a case of legal extortion. If he can get enough out of each of us to make this go away, he'll win."

"You're not going to cave in, are you?" I asked.

Moose just laughed. "I don't knuckle under to anyone, especially a cowardly extortionist. If he wants a fight, he's got one," my grandfather said as he rolled up his sleeves.

"You don't mean that literally, do you?" I asked. I wouldn't put it past Moose to take a swing at the man.

"I don't know just yet," Moose said. "Anyway, I've got to go tell Cynthia and Hank about what I found out." He then turned to Greg and asked, "Aren't you going to be late for your poker game?"

"I wasn't sure if I should go," Greg admitted.

"This is one night you can't afford to miss. See if you can drop what I found out into the conversation. It won't hurt having those men on our sides."

"Melinda, is that okay with you?" Greg asked my mother.

"Go. I've been looking forward to working with my daughter all day. Surely you wouldn't rob me of that, would you?"

He grinned as he slid out of his apron. "It's all yours."

Stopping beside me, he gave me a quick kiss, and then headed for the door.

"I always liked that young man," Moose said.

"The feeling's mutual. Go spread the word, Moose. Mom and I can handle this."

"You're a pair of fine ladies as well," he said as he hugged us both and followed after Greg.

Once he was gone, Mom said, "This place is well named, isn't it? Your grandfather really can be charming."

"He can be when he wants to be," I admitted. "So, should we get started?"

"You and Jenny bring me the orders, and I'll take care of the rest," she said as she put on her morning apron.

"That's the last of it," Mom said an hour later. "The grill's officially closed for the day. That went fast."

"It was just an hour," I reminded her. "Thanks again for covering for Greg."

"I was happy to do it," she said. The last of the dishes had been run through the wash, and Jenny had finished sweeping the front. I'd sent her home so that I could have a little time with my mother.

"Are you worried about this mess we seem to find ourselves in?" I asked her.

"Not after what Moose uncovered," she said. "Even if he hadn't found out what Howard Lance was up to, I would still have faith in him and your father to resolve this."

"They make an odd pair for a father and son, don't they?" I asked.

"I don't know. I think that in many ways, they are a great deal alike."

I nearly dropped the sweet tea I was drinking. "Excuse

me? We are talking about the same two men, aren't we?"

"Don't judge them by their outward appearances, Victoria. Both men have a strong sense of loyalty, of family, and of always standing by their word. Honor is important to them, and they take their vows seriously. In all the ways that count, they are very much cut from the same cloth."

"I can see that," I said.

Mom took off her apron and hung it from the peg that was hers. She surprised me by hugging me, and then she said, "Victoria, don't waste a minute more of worry about this. It will all turn out in the end."

"I hope you're right," I said as I noticed for the first time that the back door of the restaurant was slightly ajar.

"When did that happen?" I asked as I walked past her and tried to shut it. It caught a little, and then I pulled harder and finally managed to get it dead bolted in place. "Mom, do you know how long this door was unlocked?"

"To be honest with you, I didn't even notice it," she said. "I certainly didn't do it."

"Greg must have done it by accident," I said. "I wonder how long it's been catching like that." My husband was meticulous about keeping things locked up, and I knew that he'd be disturbed to find out what had happened. It didn't matter, though, since nothing seemed to be disturbed.

"Are you coming?" Mom asked me. "I'd be happy to walk you out."

"Thanks, but I've got to do a spot check on the freezer inventory," I said.

Mom patted my shoulder. "You don't like to go home to an empty place any more than I do, do you? I could always hang around and give you a hand, you know."

I smiled. "Thanks, but I'm a big girl. I see more than enough of my husband throughout the week to ever worry about a few hours alone at night."

Mom wouldn't return my smile, though. "Now don't you try to lie to your mother. We both know that's not true, don't we?"

I thought about continuing my bluff, but she knew me too well. "Okay, I miss my husband when he's not around. That's not a bad thing, is it?"

"On the contrary. I think it's sweet. Good night, Victoria."

"Good night," I said.

After I let her out the front and locked the door behind her, I thought about leaving myself, going home, and drawing myself a nice bath.

I wasn't ready to go yet, though. I was walking back through the restaurant when I spotted the latest mystery from Dame Sylvia Dark sitting on the seat of one of the booths. I picked it up, started to thumb through it, and then found myself caught up in the story from the first page. When I looked up two hours later, I hadn't even realized that time had passed. I started to put the book in our Lost and Found, but then decided it wouldn't hurt to take it home and finish it tonight. I promised myself a quick check of the freezer, and then I was heading home.

It didn't work out that way, though.

It took me all of thirty seconds to find the body, even though it had been stuffed in back behind a swan ice sculpture we were storing for an artist friend, a pallet of ice cream that didn't belong there, and all of our regular supplies. What had caught my eye was an old tarp that was out of place. When I lifted it to move it, I found that it was covering a body.

Thoughts of the novel I'd been reading suddenly flew out of my mind.

I had a real mystery on my hands now.

Someone had decided to end Howard Lance's threats before he had a chance to see them through, and they'd left him for us at the diner to deal with ourselves.

"Greg, is the sheriff still there with you?" I asked my husband once my hands stopped shaking long enough to dial my husband's number on my cell phone. If it hadn't been on

Speed Dial, I never would have made it all the way through seven digits. I was pretty rattled by my recent discovery, and I didn't care who knew it.

"Sure, he's sitting right here. Why do you need him? He's got seven dollars of mine that I aim to get back before the night is over." I hated to ruin my husband's good mood, but it couldn't be helped.

"Put him on the phone, Greg," I said, maybe a little harsher than I intended.

"Victoria, what's wrong?" All the playfulness was now gone from his voice.

"I don't want to have to say this twice. Please?"

"Okay," Greg said, and the next voice I heard belonged to Sheriff Edgar Croft. "What's going on, Victoria?" he asked.

"I found a body in our freezer at the diner," I said. "It's Howard Lance."

There was a slight hesitation before he responded to that, as though he wasn't at all sure that I was serious. "Come again?"

"You heard me the first time, Sheriff."

"Are you sure that he's dead?" he asked me.

I heard Greg clamoring for the phone as I said, "He's dead, and there's no doubt about it." I remembered the cold, white features I'd seen, and the frosted tips of his eyebrows when I'd found him. His skin was cold to the touch, and there was no pulse that I could find.

"Don't touch anything. I'll be right there."

"Should I call the paramedics?" I asked.

"I'll take care of it," he said.

The next thing I heard was Greg. "Victoria? Is it really true?"

"It is," I admitted. "Greg, could you come back to the diner? I need you."

"I'll be there before the sheriff gets there," he said, and then hung up before I could say anything else.

He didn't actually beat Sheriff Croft, but he did make it The Charming Moose twenty seconds before the paramedics arrived.

"You can't come in here right now, Greg," the sheriff told him as he met him at the door. I was sitting at one of the booths, wishing that I had something stronger than sweet tea in my glass. I was normally pretty much a teetotaler, but I could have used a sip of a little liquid courage at the moment.

"Just try to stop me," he said as he shoved past the sheriff.

"At least stay out of the kitchen," Croft said.

"I have no interest in going back there," he said as he slid onto the bench seat beside me and wrapped me in his arms. "Are you okay?"

The tension I'd been experiencing suddenly began to slip away from me, and I felt myself melt into my husband's arms. I was as independent as the next gal, some said even more so, but I'd be lying if I said that it didn't feel good having him hold me.

"I'm better now," I said. I pulled back and looked at him. "Greg, it was awful."

"I'm sure it was," he said. "How did he even get in there?"

I had a question to ask him, and I didn't see any way around posing it, but I had to, and before the sheriff got around to it. "Did you unlock the back door today for any reason?"

"Let's see. Yeah, I had a special delivery for the freezer about four."

"We weren't supposed to get any orders today," I said.

"Remember? I promised Larry Evans that we'd take a pallet of ice cream to hold for him while his freezer's getting fixed. He doesn't want folks to know that he's having trouble, so it's pretty hush-hush."

"With that goose ice sculpture we're keeping, too, I'm amazed that we have room for our own supplies."

"Brian Wright made it for practice a week early before Sally Ann Culver's wedding. Is it his fault that it turned out so beautifully on the day of the murder? It's a real work of art." He paused, and then added, "It's a swan, by the way, not a goose."

"I don't care if it's a replica of the Empire State Building, it's taking up too much room in our storage area."

"Why are you suddenly so interested in what's in our freezer, and when it got there?" Before I even had the chance to answer, he did it for me. "I left the back door unlocked after they brought the ice cream and the sculpture in, didn't I?"

"There was a catch in the latch when I shut it, but Greg, I'm not accusing you of anything," I said.

He shook his head as he answered, "You don't have to. I failed to lock up, and someone must have followed Lance into our freezer. Why he was there in the first place is beyond me, but what I want to know is, when did they have time to sneak in? I barely left the kitchen all day."

"Think about it. Did you ever leave the back for more than a minute or two? We know that door was unlocked between four when you took that delivery and seven when I found it and locked it back."

He considered it, and then nodded. "You and I were eating dinner out front between five and five thirty. While we were out in the dining room, someone killed Howard Lance in our freezer. Victoria, I'm never going to be able to forgive myself for this."

It was my turn to console my husband. "Greg, that's crazy, and you know it. You left a door unlocked and had dinner with your wife. You didn't have any more to do with killing Howard Lance than any of the rest of us. Whoever decided to murder him could have done it just about anywhere that the opportunity arose. The fact that they chose our freezer to make one of us look guilty just makes me angry enough to spit fire. The killer tried to put this on us on purpose, Greg, and I'm not going to stand for it."

He accepted what I said, and then nodded in agreement. "That goes double for me. This might not have been my fault, but I'm not about to let someone else try to pin a murder on someone in our family. We need to call Moose, and I mean right now."

I was about to do just that when I looked up and saw my grandfather marching quickly to the diner that had been named after him.

It appeared that we weren't the only ones who were livid about where the killer had chosen to strike.

Chapter 4

"What's the meaning of this?" Moose asked as he barged into the restaurant past the flashing lights of the police cars and the ambulance.

The sheriff was just coming out of the kitchen area, and I noticed that there was a slight hitch to his step as he turned to face my grandfather.

"There's been a murder here, Moose," he said calmly. "No one's allowed in the kitchen until my team is done in there."

"You can't tell me what to do in my own diner," my grandfather said loudly.

I decided to get between them before Moose said something that we'd all live to regret. "Leave him alone. He's just doing his job, Moose."

"Are you telling me that you're on his side?" my grandfather asked, clearly amazed by my reaction.

"I'm with you, one hundred percent, and you shouldn't even have to ask that question, but I'm the one who found the body, or did no one tell you that?"

"What?" he asked, crumpling a little. "I'm sorry. I didn't know." Moose wrapped me up in his arms much as my husband just had. It wasn't a rare response from Greg, but my grandfather wasn't much of a hugger. "Are you alright, child?" he asked softly as he stroked my head gently.

"I'm fine," I said, though it was clearly not the case. "There will be plenty of time to deal with this in our way once the police are finished here." I turned to Sheriff Croft and asked, "When will that be, exactly?"

"If I had to guess, I'd say that it will be at least twenty-four hours," he said.

Moose was about to explode again when I beat him to the punch. In as gentle a voice as I could muster given the circumstances, I asked him, "Are you sure you can't release it before that? It's how we make our living, you know."

The sheriff considered it, and then nodded. "I'll see what I can do. Maybe we can give it back to you by two o'clock tomorrow afternoon."

"Eleven would be better," Moose said strongly.

"But we'll appreciate whatever we get," I said before the sheriff could change his mind. "Moose, can I see you outside?"

"What? What can you not say in here?"

"Just come with me," I said as I took his hand. Greg raised an eyebrow in my direction, but I shook my head. I had to do this on my own.

Once we were outside, I asked, "Moose, what were you thinking just now?"

He looked surprised by my tone of voice. "What are you talking about?"

"This is not the time to bluster and bully. We need the sheriff on our side, and your demands aren't helping any. We've got to play this cool and not cause any waves. Do you understand me?"

"Nobody tells me what I can and cannot do with my diner," he stated firmly.

"Whose diner is it?" I asked softly.

"I know you're running the place now," he said reluctantly, "but don't forget, I started it in the first place."

"I'm not disputing that," I said as I put a hand on his chest. "But neither one of us can afford to have an attitude, not right now. If you can't behave yourself, you might serve the family best by going home right now and letting cooler heads prevail."

He laughed at that, not the reaction that I was expecting at all. "Are you threatening to throw me out of the diner I started, Victoria?"

"Me?" I asked as innocently as I could. "We both know that I'd never do that, Moose."

He just shook his head, but I saw that the wry smile was still there. "Fine. You've made your point, and I get the picture."

"So, you're going home?"

"Not on your life," he said with a laugh, "but I will promise to try to behave myself."

"Thank you," I said as I reached up and kissed him.

"You're a great deal like your grandmother. You know that, don't you?"

"That's just about the nicest thing you could say to me," I admitted.

"And don't I know it. Now let's get back inside before that husband of yours dies from the curiosity building up inside him."

I glanced in at the booth where Greg was still sitting and saw that he was so close to the edge of the bench seat that he was in real danger of falling off altogether. Looping my arm in Moose's, I led him back inside, and as he took a seat across from where Greg was sitting, I found my husband staring at me with something akin to awe. I winked at him, but did my best not to let Moose see it. We were all on dangerous ground at the moment, and I didn't want to do anything that might disturb the delicate balance we'd just hammered out.

Mom and Martha came into the diner a few minutes later, and we were all sitting around our largest booth when Sheriff Croft came out of the kitchen.

"I see you've called a family meeting," he said as he nodded to my mother and grandmother. "Ladies, it's nice to see you both, despite the circumstances."

"You as well," Martha said.

I thought about chiding the sheriff for not looking at me when he'd said the word 'ladies,' but then I took to heart the lecture I'd given Moose. I decided to let it slide, much to my husband's surprise. Well, it didn't hurt to throw him off every now and then, either.

"This is a terrible tragedy," my grandmother said.

"It's unfortunate," Croft agreed.

"How are you planning on getting the body out?" Moose asked.

"Moose," my grandmother said, admonishing him gently.

"Hey, it's not going to do our diner's reputation any good for any of our customers to see a corpse being wheeled out of the place, wouldn't you agree?"

"Don't worry. We've got that covered, Moose. I asked the ambulance to move around back, and after we get a few more photos and some more video footage, we'll be removing it out the back door. I'm glad you are all here. I've got some questions to ask."

"Not without an attorney present," my father said.

"Joe, we have nothing to hide," Moose said.

"I appreciate the fact that you feel that way, Dad, but I still think it couldn't hurt to be represented before we start answering questions."

My grandfather just shrugged, and then he said something under his breath.

I caught it, but I was certain my grandmother had not.

"What did you just say?" she asked Moose.

When he didn't answer, I said, "He mentioned that Holly advised the same thing."

Moose stared at me a second, and then said, "Rat."

"Hey, if you don't have the guts to repeat it, don't say it in the first place," I answered.

"Are we talking about Judge Dixon?" Sheriff Croft asked, clearly surprised by this turn of events.

"She's our legal advisor," Moose said.

"So, it appears that we're at a stalemate, Sheriff," Greg said.

He sighed loudly, and then said, "Folks, I'm not trying to railroad you all into anything. There are just some things I need to know so that I can move forward with my investigation."

"Are you offering us immunity?" my mother asked softly.

"What? No, of course not." He seemed to think about it

for a moment or two, and then said, "How about this? I'll ask you questions all at the same time. You can confer among yourselves if you'd like before you answer me. This is all pretty innocent."

"For a murder investigation, you mean?" I asked. I looked around at my family, and said, "I'm game if you all are. What do you all say?"

Everybody nodded their assent, with the exception of my father.

"Motion carried," I said, and then shot a look of condolence toward my father.

"It's on your heads," he said. "Don't say that I didn't try to warn you."

"You won't hear it from me," Moose said, which I suspected was a big fat lie. My grandfather happened to conveniently forget the things he wanted to, while remembering in perfectly crisp detail those things that fell in his favor.

"What's your first question?" I asked the sheriff.

"When did any of you last see the deceased?"

"That had to be when I found his body in the freezer," I said.

"That's not what I meant. When was the last time any of you saw him alive?"

"Hang on a second," Greg said. "Don't answer that, Victoria."

"Why not?" I asked.

"Because I think it might be easier if we just tell him what we figured out while we were sitting here together waiting for him."

I thought about it, and then nodded. "You're right. Go ahead and tell him."

Greg explained, "Sheriff, I had an ice cream drop-off earlier today around four, so I had to open the delivery door. I thought I locked it back when they left, but the latch must have caught on something, and it was still unlocked when Victoria and her mother discovered my mistake around seven."

"So, there were three hours when someone could have slipped in, killed Howard Lance, and then slipped out again."

"You've clearly never worked in a diner's kitchen," Moose said. "It's as busy as a four ring circus back here."

"Not necessarily," I said, hating to contradict my grandfather, especially when it only hurt us. "Greg and I had lunch out front from around five to five thirty. If you're looking for a time of death, I'm guessing that's going to line up pretty closely, unless the cold temperature throws off the coroner when he performs the autopsy."

"What do you know about autopsies?" the sheriff asked me.

"I read a lot, and it's eclectic," I said. "It's amazing the kind of odd tidbits I pick up. Tell me I'm wrong."

As he stroked his chin, he said, "No, I can't do that. It's most likely that your timeline is closer than anything science is going to be able to come up with, given the circumstances."

"Then we were of help to you," Mom said.

"Sure, that's good information to have," he said. "I'll rephrase my question, given what you just told me. Where were each of you between five and five thirty this afternoon?"

"I already told you. Greg and I were out here eating," I said, "and there are half a dozen folks who can testify to that. We're in the clear."

I was feeling pretty proud of myself when he said, "Not so fast. Victoria, as much as I hate to admit it, I can see another scenario playing out here."

"Go on. I'm listening," I said.

"What if Howard came in between four and five? He confronted you, you killed him, and your husband helped you stash him in the freezer. You pretended nothing happened until you conveniently discovered the body later."

"Have you completely lost your mind?" Moose asked as he started angrily toward the sheriff.

My dad was too quick for him, though. "Hang on a second, Dad. You're not going to be able to do us any good if you're sitting in a jail cell being charged with assaulting an officer of the law."

Moose turned away, and the sheriff said, "Thanks for that."

My father turned on him then, and said, "Don't thank me for anything just yet. I'd like to punch your lights out myself for implying that my daughter was involved in this in any way. You are way out of line, Sheriff, and this group interview is over."

"It's over when I say it is," Sheriff Croft said firmly.

"If you want to hold us, you'll have to arrest us," Martha said as she stood. "Family, let's go. We're leaving."

The sheriff was clearly flabbergasted by my grandmother's stand, but he made no move to stop us as we walked out together.

"This is most disturbing," Martha said. "It appears that our family is going to be at the center of the police's investigation of this murder."

"The problem is that we know that none of us did it, but it's going to be hard to prove," Greg said, and Moose put an arm around my husband's shoulder for a moment in support.

"But we have to convince them that we're innocent," my dad said. "Does anyone have any idea how we might do that?"

"It's pretty obvious, isn't it?" I asked.

"Enlighten me," Dad said.

"If nobody else is trying to solve this case without focusing on our family, then we're just going to have to do it ourselves."

There were a few murmurs of assent, and then Martha nodded. "Agreed. We'll reconvene at our house and decide on an order of business. Victoria, you're the crime fiction lover among us. Will you be the head of our unofficial investigation?"

"I'd be happy to," I said, "but solving crimes written by

novelists isn't the same as solving them in real life."

"You've got an analytical mind," Moose said. "I agree with my wife. You're the boss, at least as far as this murder investigation goes." He looked around at the others, and asked, "Are there any objections from anyone about this?"

I was proud when my entire family agreed, but I also felt the burden of this decision. It appeared that it was going to be up to me to lead this crazy group and hunt down a killer.

I just hoped that I was up to the task.

We were about to leave the diner's parking lot when the front door opened. "Hang on a second," the sheriff said.

When he joined us, he said, "I know you people, and I consider you all friends, but I don't want you digging around in this murder yourselves, do you understand me?"

"What gave you the idea that we'd do that?" I asked as innocently as I could muster.

"Like I said, I know you."

"If we want to dig into this murder, you can't stop us," Moose said, clearly irritated by the sheriff's attempt to stifle our investigation before it even got started.

"Maybe not," he said as he scratched his chin, "but you have to admit that I could make life pretty unpleasant for all of you."

"Be reasonable," I said. "We all know that we're in this up to our necks. Folks in this town like you, but there are quite a few who aren't going to give you the time of day when you start asking questions, and you know it. Why not use us instead of banning us from investigating?"

"Because none of you are trained police officers," he said, his voice getting a little heated.

"Don't you see, though? That's an advantage, in this case."

"Stop trying to appease him, Victoria. He's not going to budge, and neither am I," Moose said.

The sheriff thought about it, and then finally said, "You're not going to let me talk you out of this, are you?"

Moose stood proudly as he shook his head. We came

from a long line of dissenters, and he was doing his best to make our ancestors proud.

The sheriff looked around, and then let out a heavy sigh. "If any of you breathes a single word of this to anyone else, our deal's off. One of you, and I mean one, can do a little nosing around the edges. Stay out of my way, and I'll stay out of yours. If you find one small speck of something that might be evidence, you are to bring it directly to me. Moose, I assume that you're the one who will be investigating."

"No, sir, not me. We already voted, and Victoria's running this operation."

I didn't know how to respond to that, but I didn't have to. He turned to Greg before I could reply and asked, "Do you feel good letting your wife confront a killer all by herself?"

"She won't be alone," Greg said. "If she goes anywhere, I'm going to be right there beside her."

Moose stepped in at that moment. "Greg, I'm sure that Victoria appreciates your commitment to her, but most of the folks involved in the original deal are old codgers like me. We go way back, and I know where all of the skeletons are buried. I won't let anything happen to her. You have my word on that," he said as he stuck out his hand.

To his credit, Greg looked at me before he moved another muscle. "What do you think about that, Victoria?"

"He's right. It's got to be the two of us."

"Why can't Moose do it alone?" Greg asked.

I looked at my husband as I said, "It shouldn't come as a surprise to anyone standing here that Moose has a tendency to shoot first and ask for explanations later." I turned to my grandfather and added, "Do you disagree with that?"

"What can I say? I believe in getting straight to the point," Moose said.

"It might be an admirable trait normally," I said, "but this calls for something more subtle than a brick between the eyes. I won't do it if you don't let me ask the questions. Are we agreed?"

He took a moment, and then nodded. "That's fine."

The sheriff just shook his head. "I should be locked up for agreeing to this, but I've got a hunch that I'm going to need all of the help I can get. Do me a favor and don't do anything that risks your lives. I couldn't stand wading through the paperwork if something happened to either one of you."

He walked back inside, and I turned to the rest of my family. "I didn't mean to exclude you all, but I have a hunch the sheriff was going to withdraw his offer if I didn't agree to just the two of us investigating. Is that acceptable?"

"As it can be," Greg said as he hugged me. Mom and Dad joined in, and Martha hugged Moose.

She said soft enough for all us to hear, "If anything happens to my granddaughter, you might as well keep on going and not show your face around here ever again. Do we understand each other, Moose?"

I glanced over and saw my grandfather nodding solemnly. "Yes, Ma'am."

"Then, that's settled. Let's go home and have a brainstorming session together. Just because we can't help actively investigate doesn't mean that we can't put our heads together and come up with some kind of plan of attack."

After working together as a family late into the night, Moose and I had a list of suspects to speak with in the morning. Dad was going to work as usual, ready to help at a moment's notice if he was needed, while Greg and Mom planned to work together at our place for the same reason. While they were there waiting together in case we needed them, they were going to work on some new recipes for The Charming Moose, so it wasn't as though they would be sitting around twiddling their thumbs.

Moose and I would be tackling a pretty thorough list, one that included Hank Brewer, Cynthia Wilson, Bob Chastain, and Francie Humphries. If anyone else got our attention, we'd tackle them as well, but for the moment, we had more than enough that we had to do.

At least the diner was closed. I hated the loss of income and inconveniencing our regular patrons, but it would allow us to focus on the investigation and not worry about who would have to be there to take my place. I wasn't exactly essential to the daily operation of the diner, but I was there more than anyone else, and my presence would be missed.

Chapter 5

"Where should we start?" I asked Moose the next morning as I climbed into his battered old pickup truck. He'd come by to collect me, and I'd heard him coming with that battered old muffler of his three blocks away from the house. His truck had once been a subdued shade of red, but those days were long gone. Moose liked to repaint any faded spots or repairs with whatever can of spray paint he had on hand, and it had become a tie-dyed explosion over the years. He could have driven a brand new vehicle if he'd wanted to, but my grandfather said that this one suited him, and who was I to disagree?

"I thought we'd pop in on Francie first thing this morning," he said as he headed in the direction of her shop, a bakery she'd named simply, Iced. It allowed her to have a lot of fun with the name in the shop, decorating the windows with overblown images of snowflakes year-round. The walls and ceiling inside had been painted a uniform shade of pale blue, and white icicles had been painted randomly hanging down the sides. It almost gave you a chill when you walked inside. Fake diamonds were scattered around the place as well, with large ones the size of a man's fist glued to the register. She didn't need the cutesy theme, though; her cakes and cupcakes were known throughout most of North Carolina, and her cookies were not that far behind.

"Hello, Moose," Francie said with a nervous smile. She was my grandfather's age, short and thin, with hair that had once been blonde, but was now solidly silver. In a very real way, she'd grown to project the perfect image of her shop, with hair naturally frosted white with age. "I heard about what happened to Howard Lance. It's terrible that someone killed him in your diner."

"It had to happen someplace, I guess," Moose answered.

It was too much for me to hope that Francie hadn't heard about the murder yet. Jasper Fork was a small town, and word spread like wildfire in a drought around my home town.

"How does this affect our properties?"

"I doubt anyone will be following up on it, since it appears that Howard Lance was trying to extort money from all of us."

She looked puzzled by the news. "Does that mean the legal document he gave me wasn't real? It looked plenty authentic to me."

"The paperwork was the real deal," I said, "but the conditions of the claim weren't."

"Who would do such a wicked thing?" Francie asked, dismay showing clear on her face.

"Somebody who wanted to scare us into paying him money to make it all go away," Moose said. "When's the last time you saw the man, Francie?"

"When he delivered that paper," she said. "I guess it was two days ago. Why do you ask?"

Moose had ignored his promise to me and had gone straight to the heart of our questioning. I'd wanted to ease into it, but he'd robbed me of that option. "We're trying to figure out if anyone paid him off. If they did, maybe we can help them get their money back." That wasn't exactly true, but I needed to gauge how much of a perceived threat Howard Lance had been to our list of suspects.

"I couldn't have paid him if I'd wanted to," she said, disheartened by the admission.

"I thought you were doing well. The bakery always seems to be busy, despite the lack of customers at the moment," I said as I looked around the place.

"We do okay, but it's tough to get too far ahead selling what we do where we're located," she answered. "If we were in Charlotte or Raleigh, we'd do much better, but I never could stand big cities."

"So, just for the record, you're claiming that you didn't see him at all the day of the murder; is that right?" Moose asked. My grandfather frowned as he asked the question, as though he didn't believe her answer at all.

"I didn't!" she insisted. "And anyone who said I did is lying."

It was a pretty emphatic answer, but we weren't done yet. "If anyone could vouch for where you were yesterday from five to five thirty, it would help us all out a lot," I said calmly, trying to ease the stress in our line of questioning.

"Victoria, are you asking me for an alibi?" She clearly didn't like that at all.

"Don't feel like we're picking on you in particular. We're asking everyone Howard Lance served papers to," I said. Technically that wasn't true yet, but it was going to be by the time we finished.

"Since when did you two start solving crimes?" she asked.

"Since the murder happened in the back of our diner," Moose said bluntly. His voice left no room for doubt about where we stood, and why we felt as though we had the right to be asking these questions. "So, what's it going to be? Are you going to help us, or not?"

"I'll help you," she said. "But what I've got to say won't do you much good. I'm afraid I was getting ready for the Hampton girl's ninth birthday party," she said.

"So, they can verify that you were there?" I asked, relieved at how easy this was.

"No," she said with a frown. "I was working on the cupcakes in back, and I'm sorry to say that I was all by myself. They wanted the most hideous shade of green for the icing, and I had the devil's own time getting it just right. That doesn't mean that I killed that man, though, no matter how much he deserved it!"

"That's a little strong of a reaction for a little bit of extortion, Francie," Moose said.

"You know what I mean," she said, the anger clear in her voice now.

It was time to see if we could get out of there without

damaging our relationship with her forever. "Thanks for cooperating with us, Francie. We got what we came for, and we're sorry to trouble you," I said as I tugged on my grandfather's arm. "Come on, Moose."

"What? I'm not in any hurry to leave just yet." He was digging in his heels, and I had to move him along while I still could.

"We're finished, though," I said, trying to get him to go.

"You might be, but I want to try one of those apple pie cupcakes," he said as he pointed at the display case.

"Do you think Martha would approve of you sampling treats here?" I asked him. The entire family knew that my grandmother kept him on a pretty tight leash as far as his diet was concerned, but Moose didn't tend to let that stop him, especially if she wasn't around to slap his hand.

"What she doesn't know won't hurt her," he said as he smiled at Francie and handed her a five. "We'll take two."

As she started to get them, I said, "Make it one, instead. We'll split it."

"I'm a big boy, young lady. I can eat a whole cupcake by myself."

"Indulge me," I said.

"Fine. One cupcake but split it in half." He hesitated and then grinned. "Forget that. I want three quarters of it for myself."

Francie looked at me, and I reluctantly nodded my approval.

We took her offerings, and I had a bite of mine. It was amazing how she'd gotten the essence of an apple pie into a cupcake, from the crumb topping laced in the icing to the apple chunks in the body of the cupcake itself. My section was gone much too quickly, and I could see where Moose's original idea had merit, but I decided that I'd better get him out of there before I let him change my mind. By the time we left, we were on pretty good terms with Francie again, and I could see the logic behind my grandfather's purchase.

"I see what you just did in there," I said with a smile once we were out on the sidewalk again.

"I tried to order two cupcakes and got a partial instead," he said grumpily. "There was nothing clever about that."

"You put Francie at ease after you riled her up."

He shrugged. "Where do you think we got the 'charming' part of the diner's name? What's your gut tell you about Francie? Could she have killed Howard Lance?"

"I don't know. She seems kind of timid, doesn't she? Do you honestly think that she had the nerve to creep into our freezer, kill Howard Lance, and sneak back out again? I'd think that it would take someone with a lot steadier nerve than she has to do it."

"Don't let her demeanor fool you," Moose said. "You back somebody up into a corner, and you never know how they'll behave. I'd like to know if anyone in town saw her around Howard Lance yesterday at all, since there's no way to shake her alibi that she was working in back alone. If we could get someone to say that they saw them together at any point, that would break her story wide open."

"So then, we file her away for now and move onto our next suspects," I said. "Should it be Cynthia, Hank, or Bob?"

"Well, Bob Chastain is just around the corner. Why don't I tackle him next?"

The implication was clear in his voice that he wanted to go alone, but I wasn't going to stand for that. "Moose, we're a team, remember?"

"I know that, but Bob might talk a little more openly with me if it's just the two of us." The defiance was clear in the way he was standing, but it wasn't going to do him one bit of good.

"That's just too bad," I said. "Moose, if you try to do this alone, I'm going straight to the sheriff."

"You'd rat me out to the cops, my own flesh and blood?"

His guilt trip wasn't going to work on me. "You know I would. I'm just as tough as you are, old man."

"Who are you calling old?" Moose said with a grin, now that I'd stood up to him. As he ran a hand through his silver hair, he said, "I'm just now getting aged to perfection."

"I'm going to let you have that one. Come on. Let's go see Bob."

As we drove toward the auto shop, Moose grinned over at me. "Where'd you get all that spunk, young lady?"

"I inherited it from my grandfather," I said proudly.

"You bet you did." He parked the truck out front of the shop, and the two of us walked in together.

"Moose, what's the big idea?" Bob asked as he came out of his office.

"What do you mean?" my grandfather asked. Had Francie already talked to him about our line of questioning? We were counting on hitting them all by surprise, and I might have underestimated the power of our local grapevine.

"How am I going to get any customers if that wreck of yours is parked out front?" he asked with a broad grin.

Moose said, "Are you kidding? You should pay me to park in front of your shop."

"How do you see it that way?" Bob asked. He'd recently lost a ton of weight by easing off the fast food and walking during his lunch breaks, and the man looked ten years younger these days.

"Think of it this way. If it looks as though you can keep my truck running, you can do anything," Moose said proudly.

"At least let me paint it," Bob said.

"What, and ruin its charm? No thank you."

"I give up," Bob said as he threw his hands up in the air. "If you're not here about the truck, what can I do for you?"

"We're trying to find out who killed that weasel Victoria found in our freezer," he said bluntly. I was going to have to have another talk with my grandfather about who was really leading this investigation.

"I heard about that," Bob said as he nodded. "So, you're trying to earn your junior crime buster Boy Scout merit badge, is that it?"

"Do you blame us?" I asked.

"No, I guess I don't. Sorry, but I can't help you."

"But you had as much reason as we did to want to stop the man, didn't you?" I asked.

"Victoria, I don't need this particular piece of land to work on cars. I could set up somewhere else in a week if I had to. Folks come for my service, not my surroundings."

"Come on, don't kid a kidder," Moose said. As he swept his arm around the place, he said, "Even relocating this stuff doesn't come cheap, and besides, I've never known you to back down from a fight in your life."

"I could say the same about you," Bob said as he stared at Moose.

"What, do you think I did it?" my grandfather asked.

"No more than I did," he said.

"Where were you when he was killed?" Moose asked.

"I didn't know they had a time of death yet. Doesn't being stuffed in a freezer kind of throw off those forensics people?"

"How do you know about that?" I asked.

"Hey, I watch television. You can't turn the channel without hitting one of those crime shows these days."

"Unfortunately, this isn't fiction," Moose said.

"I know that, but my point's still a fair one."

It was time to fess up to what had happened. "We left the back door unlocked by accident, and Greg and I were eating an early dinner when it had to have happened. Our closest guess is between five and five thirty."

"Wow, that's pretty unfortunate," Bob said with a frown.

"So, what's your alibi?" Moose asked again.

"I'll tell you mine if you tell me yours," Bob said with an expression that told me he wasn't kidding.

"I just told you. I was out front eating with Greg," I said.

"I wasn't talking to you," he answered, never taking his eyes off of Moose.

"I was in my woodworking shop," Moose said.

"Alone?" Bob asked.

"Sure, I was by myself, but Martha must have heard me using my table saw."

"So, you just have your wife to vouch for you," Bob said. "I wish I had even that much. It figures. The one time I slip out of the shop to have a little fun, it bites me in the rear."

"Where were you?" I asked.

"I slipped over to Hickory to see an early movie," he admitted. "They're cheaper if you go before six."

"Can anyone vouch for that?" Moose asked.

"I wish. I got halfway there and turned around. I had burritos from Carmelita's on the way, and something I ate didn't agree with me, so I turned around and came back home."

"Then your receipt should prove that you weren't in town," I said.

"It might if I'd bought them fresh, but these had been leftover in the fridge for a few days, so I didn't buy them fresh yesterday. I'm sad to say that no one saw me between five and five thirty, coming or going."

I was about to ask him another question when one of his mechanics came in. "Bob, your car's transmission is shot. Why don't you just shoot that thing and put it out of its misery?" He waved to Moose, and nodded in my direction.

"It's got a few good miles left on it," Bob said. "Just fix it."

"If you're having trouble with your transportation," Moose said, "I might sell you my truck. It's good to go right now, just as it is."

"Thanks, but you'll understand if I pass."

His mechanic said, "One more thing. Mrs. Beatty is back by my station. She swears that we changed the seats of her car the last time she was here, and they haven't been right since. You might want to have a chat with her."

Bob shook his head, and then turned to us. "Sorry, but duty calls. Good luck in your witch-hunt."

"We're not on some kind of rampage. We're just trying to find the truth," I said.

"Call it whatever you want," Bob said, and then he followed his mechanic back out to the work area.

"What do you think about that?" I asked as soon as we were back in Moose's truck.

"It sounds like a pretty elaborate story, if it's all just a lie," he said.

"Or it could actually be the truth," I answered.

"Maybe, but I'm not buying Bob's story that this didn't upset him, no matter how hard he's trying to downplay it. If he went to a movie in Hickory after finding out that he might be losing his garage, I'm a baboon's first cousin."

"He never made it though, remember?"

"So he says," Moose said.

"How long have you known the man?" I asked, more out of curiosity than anything else.

"Longer than I've known you," he admitted with a smile.

"And you really think that he's capable of doing this?"

"I sure do, and there's no doubt in my mind that he thinks the same thing of me. We need to keep digging into this, Victoria. There's going to be a lot of bad blood before this thing is over."

"I agree," I said as my cell phone rang. I glanced at the caller ID and saw that Greg was calling me. "Drive us to Cynthia's or Hank's. I need to talk to my husband in the meantime."

As I answered the call, my grandfather said, "You know that I hate those things."

"I know," I said as I grinned at him and answered my phone. "Hey there, Greg. Did you miss me already?"

"Always," my husband said, "but that's not why I'm calling. The sheriff's looking for you two. He wants you both to stop whatever you're doing and meet him at the diner."

I didn't like the sound of that. "Did he say what it was about?" I was afraid that he'd already heard about our digging this morning, and was going to shut us down before we got the chance to do any good with our investigation.

"No, but from his tone, I wouldn't put it off any longer than you have to."

"We'll head over there right now. Thanks for calling."

"Let me know when you find out what this is all about," he said.

"I promise," I said, and then hung up.

"What was that all about?" Moose asked.

"Drive to the diner. Sheriff Croft is looking for us."

"Did he say why?" Moose asked.

"No, but I've got a feeling that we're about to find out."

Moose's face clouded up. "If he thinks we're going to stop looking into this murder, he's got another think coming."

"Let me handle him, okay?"

Moose shot a quick look at me. "Victoria, don't you think I'm capable of dealing with him myself?"

"Sure you are, but let's not jump the gun. Maybe this is about something else entirely."

"Granddaughter, do you believe that for one second?"

I had to admit, "No, but there's a chance, isn't there? If we go into this meeting as though we did nothing wrong, we won't blow whatever chance we have to keep at it."

"I don't like keeping my head down," Moose said, one of the biggest understatements I'd ever heard him utter in his life.

"I'm not that big a fan of it either, but it doesn't do us any good if we go in there protesting before we find out what this is all about. We both need to hold our tongues until we hear what the man has to say."

Moose grinned at me. "I can do it if you can."

"You don't think that I can keep my mouth shut if I want to?"

"I think you probably can. I've just never seen the circumstances where you felt as though you needed to."

I wanted to protest, but I couldn't. I laughed as I said, "You got me. Come on. Let's quit guessing and go find out what's up."

Chapter 6

"There you are," Sheriff Croft said when we walked into the diner a few minutes later.

"You wanted to see us?" I asked.

"I thought you might like to know that you can have your diner back early," he said as he handed me my keys back. He'd taken them the night before, promising to return them when he and his staff finished investigating the murder scene, but he'd led me to believe that I wouldn't be getting them back any time soon.

"You're really done with the place?" I asked as I glanced at my watch. It was just a little after ten, and Moose and I had two more people left to interview.

"Why do I get the sense that you're not happy about this?" the sheriff asked. "I kept two men here all night examining the place from top to bottom. I thought I was doing you a favor."

"You did," Moose said as he took my keys for me. "Great job, Sheriff. Did you find anything while you were searching the place?"

"Nothing that I'm ready to share with you," he said, and then studied us both for a second or two before adding, "Should I ask you the same question?"

"We've barely had time to scratch the surface," I said. "You didn't rush getting the diner back to us just so we couldn't investigate, did you?"

"Would I do that?" he asked with a grin. "Anyway, the place is yours."

"Would you at least tell us what killed him?" Moose asked softly.

I thought for a second that he wasn't going to answer, but after a brief moment, the sheriff said, "Somebody hit him the back of the head with a roll of frozen hamburger."

"Wow, that must have taken a pretty good swing," I said,

trying not to imagine what had happened, but failing miserably. It couldn't have been the most pleasant way to die.

"You'd be surprised how delicate the human skull is," the sheriff said.

"Well, at least the killer had to be pretty tall to do it," I said.

Moose and the sheriff both looked at me oddly, so I added quickly, "It just makes sense, doesn't it? Howard Lance wasn't a short man by any means, so if someone hit him in the head, they had to be pretty tall themselves, wouldn't they?"

The sheriff shook his head, so I asked, "Why are you acting that way? Am I wrong?"

"Ordinarily I'd say no, but the thing is, from the angle of impact, Howard must have been leaning over to tie a loose shoelace when he got clobbered. I'm sorry to say that anyone could have done it."

"That's too bad," I said.

"What, the fact that someone murdered him, or that the circumstances haven't eliminated anyone?" he asked.

I was about to answer when his radio went off. He answered it, and I glanced at Moose, who was grinning at me. I'd have to ask him what that was about after Sheriff Croft was gone.

"Sorry, I'd love to stay and chat, but I've got to run," he said.

"Is it about the case?" Moose asked.

"No, some idiot decided to try to beat a train to a crossing on the edge of town. Nobody got hurt, but this fool's car is totaled."

After the sheriff was gone, I asked my grandfather, "What was that smile about?"

"I was just impressed with the way you figured that out," he said. "How did you do it?"

"Hey, read enough mysteries, and you too can be a crime solver."

"Seriously, that's good work," Moose said. "We chose our fearless leader wisely."

"I appreciate the compliment, but we're still no closer to finding the killer than we were before," I said.

"That's why we keep digging," he said.

"What about the diner?" I asked.

"The rest of the family can pitch in today. You and I have a murder to solve." He grinned again, and added, "Besides, I've got a hunch that Greg and your mother would jump at the chance to work together for awhile. Why don't you give Ellen a call and see if she'll come in? While you're doing that, I'll round up the rest of the troops, and then we can get back to our investigation."

"That sounds like a plan to me," I said as I called my morning server at home to give her the good news.

Moose and I left the diner in the capable hands of the rest of our family a little later, and we went off in search of a killer.

When we got to The Clothes Horse, though, we found the front door locked and the CLOSED sign in the window.

"What's going on?" I asked as we got out of Moose's truck. I looked at the store hours posted by the door and saw that Hank should have been open for half an hour by now.

"I don't know, but I'm going to find out. Let's take a drive over to Hank's place and see what's going on."

When we got there, though, there was no sign of life.

It appeared that Hank was gone.

"It doesn't look good, him running like this. Doesn't he know that?" I asked Moose as he pounded on the front door for the fourth time. I didn't figure it would do him any good to keep trying, but on the other hand, it couldn't hurt, either.

"The fool must have lost his mind," Moose said, pausing for a moment.

"Do you think he might have killed Howard Lance?" I asked.

"I don't know what to think at this point, to be honest

with you."

"You just said that he had to have lost his mind."

"Victoria, I was talking about him leaving town. Just because he's gone doesn't mean that he's the killer."

"Somebody murdered that man," I said. "Why couldn't it have been Hank? His wife started this store herself, and when she died, he took it over. Maybe the thought of losing the last part he still had of her was too much for him to take."

"It's possible," Moose admitted.

"Think about it. What if your roles were reversed? Wouldn't you miss Martha at least that much?"

"Of course I would, but I'd like to think that I still wouldn't kill somebody over it."

I had my doubts myself. Moose's charm had a flipside, and that was his temper. He liked to think of it as passion, but my family knew better.

"So, what do we do about this? Do we call Sheriff Croft and tell him what we suspect, or keep it all to ourselves?"

"We could call Croft," Moose said, "but let's give Hank a chance to come back on his own before we do anything rash."

"We aren't holding anything back from him, though, remember?"

"Victoria, if Hank's on his list of suspects, the sheriff most likely already knows about this."

"And if he's not?" I asked, refusing to give any ground. We'd made a promise, and I meant to keep it.

"Tell you what. We'll go see Cynthia, and then we'll try here again. If he hasn't popped up by then, I'll call Croft myself. Is that a deal?" he asked me as he stuck out his hand.

"It's a deal," I said, taking it and doing my best to give him a solid grip in return. Moose had taught me as a small girl to give as good as I got, and I'd practiced on tennis balls until I had a grasp that came close to matching his own.

At least Cynthia was working in her hair salon when we got there. Thankfully no customers were there at the moment, though I doubted she felt that way about it. I didn't want an audience for the conversation we were about to have.

"This isn't good, is it?" she asked as Moose and I as we walked into A Cut Above.

"What makes you say that?" I asked.

"By all rights, you should be at the diner, Victoria, and Moose, you would most likely be out on a lake somewhere fishing if everything was all right."

"It's too cold for that," Moose said.

"We both know better than that," she said with a smile. "Are you both here about the murder?"

"You've heard about it already, then?" I asked.

"Oh, yes. As I was opening the doors for the day, Margie Collins came by and filled me in. She embellished it all, of course, but the gist of it was that somebody killed that worm of a man Howard Lance in your diner."

"Actually, it was the freezer, but that's about right."

"It must look bad on your family," Cynthia said.

"That's why we're trying to find the killer," Moose blurted out.

"You two? What makes you think you're capable of doing anything remotely like that?"

"We really don't have much choice," I said. "You can help us, if you're willing."

"I'll do what I can," Cynthia said, "but it's just like I told you before, Mom doesn't remember much about buying the place. If you'd like her number, I've got it here on my phone."

"Evelyn never did have all that good a memory," Moose said. "Besides, it's you we want to talk to about it."

"What do you think I can tell you that you don't already know, if you don't mind me asking?"

"Where were you yesterday between five and five thirty?" I asked. "If you've got an alibi, we can mark your name off our list."

"I'm not a suspect, am I?" she asked, her voice growing with confusion. "Why would I kill Howard Lance?"

"To save your livelihood," I said. "He was threatening to

take away all of our businesses. We're naturally the prime suspects."

"I can see the police acting that way, but we shouldn't be turning on each other," she said.

"It's not that hard a question, Cynthia," Moose said as he took a step toward her. He was a big man, and he hadn't gotten that nickname for nothing. My grandfather could be intimidating when he wanted to be, as I well knew from experience.

She was considering her options when the front door of her place opened. I was ready to push through until we had an answer, but that plan changed almost immediately when I saw that it was Sheriff Croft walking in.

"Neither one of you look as though you're getting a haircut," the sheriff said. "What brings you here?"

I was trying to come up with a safe answer that wouldn't make the sheriff irritated with us when Cynthia stole the opportunity from me to spin it in our direction. "They think I killed Howard Lance," she blurted out.

"We never said anything of the sort," I replied quickly.

"You asked me for my alibi," Cynthia said, her tone of voice accusing us of far worse.

"I need to see you two outside. Now," the sheriff said as he pointed in our direction.

"We didn't—" was all I got out. The glare he shot at me was enough to stop a rushing bull, and I didn't need to be scolded twice.

Once we were outside, Moose said, "Before you start lecturing us, Victoria was trying to tell you the truth. We were just looking for an alibi so we could strike her name off our suspect list."

"Why do you think I'm here?" the sheriff said. "Believe it or not, I've been doing this for a long time, a great deal longer than the two of you when you decided to try to solve this case yourselves. Let me guess. She wouldn't give you an answer, would she?"

"She was about to when you barged in," Moose said.

"That's not entirely the truth," I said, and my grandfather glared at me.

"We don't know that she wasn't about to spill it all, Victoria, and you know it."

"Do you honestly think that she was going to tell us anything?"

Moose just shrugged. "You never know."

"Maybe not, but I have a pretty good idea."

The sheriff stepped between us. "I told you that you could dig into this as long as you both stayed out of my way. What happened to that promise you made?"

"Hang on," I said, shifting gears immediately. "How were we supposed to know what you were up to? Send us your schedule, and we'll do our best to avoid you in the future."

Moose liked that, and he grinned at me and added a wink. I didn't return it, mainly because I was still intent on pinning the sheriff down on his last comment. We weren't mind-readers, so how could we have known what he was going to do next?

"Yeah, that's not going to happen," he said. "Come on, confess. Where have you been so far?"

I wasn't about to answer him right away, but Moose surprised me by telling him the total and unvarnished truth. "We've been to see Francie Humphries, Bob Chastain, Cynthia here, and Hank Brewer."

The last name certainly got his attention. "Are you saying that you've talked to Hank today?"

"No," Moose admitted grudgingly. "He took off before we had a chance to corner him. I take it that Hank's on your list, too."

"He was in the middle of the pack early this morning, but I have to admit, him leaving town at the spur of the moment like that shot him quite a bit closer to the top."

"But he's still behind my family, is that it?" I asked.

"I'm not ready to release the order of my suspects. Everyone's a candidate in my book."

"Then you figured out the link between Howard Lance and the rest of us?" I asked.

"Extortion," he said simply.

"He didn't have a case, you know," Moose said. "It was all done fair and legal back when we all bought land from Joshua. Howard Lance was just trying to rattle our cages a little and get someone to pay up fast before we found out that he was just scamming us."

"And did he?" the sheriff asked. "I heard about the missing deed book, and how several folks don't have receipts for buying their land. It could easily be a motive for murder."

I had to give Sheriff Croft props for figuring that all out so quickly, doing it without our inside information. "All we can say for sure is that our family didn't pay him," I said.

"What did the other folks say when you asked them about it? Were you able to get anyone's alibi?" the sheriff asked, clearly interested in our answers.

I went down my list. "Francie said that she was working on cupcakes in the back by herself, while Bob claimed that he drove to Hickory and back alone without stopping to talk to anyone on the way. We couldn't find Hank, and Cynthia won't tell us anything. Maybe you can sweat it out of her, but we weren't having any luck at all when you showed up."

"You've done some pretty good work," the sheriff said as he nodded. "You only missed one other potential suspect, as far as I'm concerned."

"I still refuse to believe that a member of my family had anything to do with this mess," I said.

"That wasn't who I was talking about," he said.

"So, we're not suspects?" I asked.

"I'm not saying that, either."

"Then who's your mystery suspect?" Moose asked.

It was pretty clear that the sheriff was reluctant to name names, so I asked, "How can we keep from stepping on your toes if we don't know what you're doing? All we need is a name."

He thought about that, and then shrugged. "Okay, but it goes no farther. Margie Collins is the last name on my list."

I could barely believe that I'd just heard that. Margie was a gray-haired widow, a Sunday School teacher, and though she loved to gossip, I couldn't imagine her as a murderer.

Moose beat me to the protest, though. "Margie? You've got to be kidding."

Sheriff Croft looked miserable as he admitted, "I wish I were, but somebody claims they saw Margie with the victim not two hours before he was murdered. I don't have much choice, do I?"

"What would she be doing with him?"

"I'd love to ask her that myself, but she's missing as well."

Chapter 7

"She took off like Hank did?" I asked. "Is there any chance that they're together?"

Moose looked at me as though I'd lost my mind, but the sheriff killed that expression when he nodded. "As hard as it is to believe, it turns out that it's possible."

I tried to imagine Margie and Hank together, but I just couldn't wrap my head around the prospect. "I didn't even know that they were dating."

"Nobody else in town did, either," Moose said.

"How could you possibly know that?" the sheriff asked him.

"Do you think they'd be able to keep that kind of secret from all of us? I'd have to see a photo of them together before I'd ever consider it a possibility."

I slapped my grandfather's shoulder. "Eww."

"I just meant in the same frame of the picture. Get your mind out of the gutter, granddaughter." He then turned to the sheriff. "What makes you think they were together?"

"I can't reveal my sources," he said, "but I believe the information is credible."

"Funny," Moose said, "but if it were anybody else, I'd go to Margie to find out what she'd heard. So, who's the number two gossip in Jasper Fork?"

"Do you mean besides you?" the sheriff asked with a hint of a grin.

I could see that Moose was about to explode, so I knew that I had to defuse the situation, and fast. "Moose isn't a gossip; he's a collector of town information. Isn't that right?" I asked him with a wink that I hoped the sheriff hadn't seen.

He took the hint. "It's true that I like to stay abreast of what's going on in my town," Moose said. "I make a fair point of it, though. If I didn't know about it, I doubt that it ever happened."

The sheriff wasn't going to accept that at face value, but it was clear that he wasn't looking to pick a fight, either.

"I'm going to go have a chat with Cynthia. Where are the two of you going next?"

"Back to the diner," I said before Moose could say a word.

The sheriff clearly had a hard time believing that we were giving up, even if it was only temporary. "What's wrong, are there no more clues for you to chase down?"

"We're set at the moment," Moose said. "And besides, our family needs us back at the diner to get things back in shape." There was very little truth to that, but I wasn't about to dispute it. I was sure that the crew we had in place was getting along swimmingly.

"Don't forget," the sheriff said as he headed back inside the salon, "let me know if you hear from Hank or Margie, or if anything else comes up that might be important."

I saluted him with a smile. "We will."

After he was gone, I turned to Moose. "Are we really going back to the diner right now?"

"We are," he said. "I'm hungry, two of our suspects are missing, and the ones we already talked to didn't give us much of anything."

"That's how it goes sometimes," I said.

"Is that your official opinion?" he asked me with a grin as we got back into his truck.

"You can quote me on it. I have to admit, I miss not running the front of the diner," I said when I saw that it was nearing eleven, the start of one of my shifts.

"You need a life, young lady," Moose said.

"I've got one, and it's a pretty good one, if you ask me. Come on, I'll make sure you eat the first thing when we get there."

"We'll both eat," Moose said. "We can chat while we're doing it and see what our next step should be."

I was hungry, and also completely out of any new ideas about what we should do next. It was one of our family's mottos that when all else failed, grab a quick bite, and things might just get better on their own. I doubted that it would work this time, but at the very least, I'd get a meal out of it before I got back to work trying to solve Howard Lance's murder.

After a bowl of Greg's chicken noodle soup and a grilled cheese sandwich, I told Moose, "I might as well take over the register until we can come up with something else to investigate."

"As a team, I'm sorry to say that we're turning out to be a real bust."

"I wouldn't say that," I countered. "We managed to learn more than Sheriff Croft was able to in such a short amount of time."

"Yeah, but we're already tapped out of ideas," he said. "What would one of those books you love be like if it all ended in chapter three?"

"Not very good," I admitted.

"Then think about where else we can look," Moose said. "Don't treat this as a real murder. Think of it as a puzzle to solve."

I did as my grandfather asked, and started playing around with what we'd learned so far, and what else we might be able to find out. "Well, I suppose we should be willing to entertain the notion that whoever killed Howard Lance wasn't from around Jasper Fork."

"What do you mean?"

"Think about it, Moose. Whoever killed him may have followed him here and done it in town. It makes perfect sense, when you look at it that way. If he was murdered around these parts, especially after the way he'd been acting, nobody would give it much credence that the most viable suspects weren't from Jasper Fork."

"Where was the man from?"

"I don't know, but I've got an idea." I went into the kitchen and retrieved the document Howard Lance had served us with such a short time before.

"What's going on?" Greg asked as he flipped a burger on the grill with skill and a little panache.

"I'm not ready to say just yet," I answered as I walked back past him.

"Be sure to let me know when you are," he said with a smile, and then turned his attention to the next order in line.

"What have you got that for?" Moose asked with distaste when he saw the legal document in my hands.

"It's our next lead."

"I don't see how," my grandfather said.

"Think about it, Moose. A lawyer wrote this up. Let's find him and see what he has to say about Howard Lance's behavior. We might just be able to uncover a whole new list of suspects."

"Victoria, I've been around a whole lot longer than you have. Getting a lawyer to admit anything, especially about a client, is as easy as turning chili into borscht."

"Even if the client's dead?"

"The first answer they learn to give is always no," Moose said.

"Well, it's at least worth trying." I looked at the document and saw that it had been drawn up by someone named M.T. Ingram in Laurel Landing.

"That's less than half an hour from here," Moose said. "I guess it's worth a try."

"That's the spirit. Let's go," I said.

"Okay by me," he answered. Instead of heading for the front door, though, I popped my head back into the kitchen before we left.

"We're following up on another lead," I told Greg, and then looked around. "Hey, I thought you and Mom were working together today."

"She had an errand to run," Greg admitted. "It's okay. I don't mind."

I had a hunch that two cooks in one kitchen was one cook too many, but I didn't say anything about it. "I'll see you later."

"Tracking down a new lead?" he asked.

"Hopefully," I replied and hesitated long enough to give him a quick kiss.

I stopped at the table on the way back and looked for the paper we'd been served with, but it was gone. What had happened to it?

I was about to panic when I looked at Moose. He was dangling the document in the air.

"You might not want to just leave this sitting around," he said when I rejoined him.

"I figured you'd have it," I answered. "Let's go to Laurel Landing and see what Mr. Ingram has to say."

We made the drive in good time, and I used my cell phone to find Ingram's address. The law office was easy enough to spot, since it was right across the street from the courthouse.

"Let me do the talking this time," Moose said. "I speak attorney. This is probably some crusty old man with cigar burns on his tie, and we can relate to each other."

"You can try, but don't think for one second that I'm going to let you go in there without me, Moose."

"Just watch and learn, youngster," Moose said as he knocked on the front door.

There was no reply, so he tried the front door, which was unlocked.

In the front office, we found a nice looking brunette woman younger than me, dressed in gray slacks and a black blouse.

"We're here to see Ingram," Moose said to the woman, clearly expecting to be ushered straight back into the inner sanctum.

She glanced at the open appointment book on the desk. "Funny, but I don't see anyone listed on the schedule today."

"I prefer this to be confidential. I'm sure your boss will

understand, and if you don't let us see him, he's not going to be very happy with you, I can promise you that."

"Know him well, do you?" the woman asked, not intimidated by my grandfather at all.

"I know enough. Let's just say that he'll want to hear what I've got to share as soon as possible," Moose answered. It was clear that he was trying to get past the receptionist, the attorney's only line of defense.

She leaned back and put her heels on the desk instead of being the slightest bit intimidated. "Well, at least you've got my attention."

I got it instantly, but Moose clearly didn't grasp it yet. He said, "I'm not going to prove the value of what I've got to say to you. Let me talk to your boss."

"If you won't give me any idea what this about, then I'm afraid I can't help you," she said firmly.

"Moose," I said as I tugged at his arm.

"Not now, Victoria." He was irritated by my interruption, but the woman simply found it amusing.

"You might want to listen to her," she said with a smile.

"What is it?" Moose asked as he stared at me.

Instead of answering him, I walked over to the woman and stuck out my hand. "M.T. Ingram, I presume?"

A broad smile spread out on her face. "At your service. And you are?"

"I'm Victoria Branson, and that gentleman over there slowly turning red with embarrassment is my grandfather, Moose Nelson."

Her smile died instantly at my grandfather's last name. "I'm sorry, but it's not appropriate for us to be speaking."

"Howard Lance is dead. Has anyone told you that?" I asked softly.

"What? Are you certain?" She was clearly surprised by my news.

"Feel free to call around and check," I said.

"I'll be right with you," Ms. Ingram said as she disappeared into her office.

When she was gone, I turned to Moose. "That was smooth, Moose. Thanks for the lesson in how to deal with people. I should have taken notes."

"How was I supposed to know that Ingram was a woman?" Moose asked. "If she's really the attorney, why was she sitting behind the receptionist's desk?"

"I don't know, but you can ask her yourself when she comes back."

"No, thanks," Moose said. He chewed his lower lip for a moment, and then asked, "Would it help if I apologized?"

I was surprised to hear his offer, but I had a hunch that it no longer mattered. "Let's just see what she has to say first."

"I like that plan," Moose admitted. He wasn't a big fan of handing out apologies, no matter how much they were merited, and I knew that it would have been tough on him doing it.

Three minutes later, Ms. Ingram came out of her office, a troubled expression on her face. "Our chief of police just confirmed the news. I'm sorry, but I'm still not at liberty to disclose anything that passed between my client and me." There was something in her glance that told me she wanted to help, but was bound by her ethics.

"We get it," Moose said as he started for the door. "It's just like I told you, Victoria. This was just another dead-end."

I had a hunch, though. "You go on without me. I'll be right out," I said.

My grandfather wasn't at all pleased with my suggestion, but when he looked at me, I narrowed my eyes, and to my delight, he did as I asked and kept going out the front door.

Ms. Ingram studied me a moment after he was gone, and then she said, "I'm really sorry, but I meant what I said. I can't disclose anything about Mr. Lance or the business I might have had with him."

"Understood," I said as I took a step forward and held out my hand. "Sorry we got off on the wrong foot. As I said, my name is Victoria, but I didn't catch your name in that barrage of initials you use."

"I'm Monica," she said as she took it. "I find the initials are useful at times."

"I have no trouble believing that."

"By the way, I love the way you handled your grandfather."

I had to smile at that. "Oh, Moose is pretty harmless if you know what you're doing."

She shook her head. "I doubt that. He reminds me a lot of my grandfather, and there's not a week goes by that I don't miss him. You're lucky to still have him."

"It doesn't always feel that way, but I know what you mean. Do you mind if I ask you a nosy question?"

"That depends. Does it have anything to do with Mr. Lance?"

"No Ma'am," I said.

"Then I'm game."

"You're clearly very good at what you do, so I'm curious. What made you set up practice here?"

She offered the hint of a smile as she explained, "I was born just outside of town, and when I left for Duke, I had grand dreams, but this place kept calling to me, and as soon as I finished law school, I came back home. There's just something about small town life, isn't there?"

"I know. I couldn't imagine ever leaving Jasper Fork. Monica, I need some advice."

"That will cost you a dollar," she said with a slight smile.

"You actually charge for giving people directions?" I asked.

"If you want our conversation to be just between us, pay me the retainer and I'm all yours."

I smiled as I handed her a buck. "Those are pretty good rates for a Duke graduate."

She scribbled out a receipt and handed it to me. "What can I say? You caught me on a good day. Now, how can I help you?"

"I understand that you can't talk about your relationship

with Howard Lance, but I was wondering if you might tell me where I might go to get a few answers."

"In general, you mean?" she asked, clearly leading me in that direction.

"Of course. Any overlap of information would strictly be a coincidence."

"Well, I've always found that if there's something I want to know about anyone in a town that's new to me, I head over to the restaurant closest to the town square."

Was she trying to tell me something? It was time to probe a little more. "And if we were discussing Laurel Landing?"

"Oh, I'd say the BBQ Pit would be the place to go." She gave me a simple set of directions, and I knew that we'd have no trouble finding it.

"Good," I said. "We'll do that. Is there anything else I should know before I go stumbling blindly around looking for information?"

"Well, folks around here are pretty willing to chat, especially if they know why they're being asked questions. Women in particular might be your best bet." It was clear she was straining to stay within her boundaries, and still somehow help us. This was the kind of woman I liked.

"Do you happen to know Rebecca Davis?" I asked on a whim. "She's an attorney in Jasper Fork."

"We've never met, but I've heard good things about her," Monica said.

"You should look her up when you get the chance. She's my best friend, and I have a feeling that the two of you would get along just fine."

"I'll make it a point," she said. "I wish I could do more, Victoria, but I'm afraid I can't say much else."

"I totally get it," I said as I offered her my hand again. "Monica, it was a pleasure to meet you."

"The same, right back at you. And don't forget, I'm on retainer now, so if you need me, I'm just a phone call away."

I thought she was half joking, but I accepted the offered

card from her just the same. While I had Rebecca to handle any jams I might find myself in, it couldn't hurt having another attorney on my side if I needed her.

"You should come by our diner sometime and I'll treat you to a free meal," I said.

"I might just take you up on it. What's it called?"

"The Charming Moose," I said, "all evidence you've seen so far to the contrary."

"Oh, I can believe he's charming enough when he puts his mind to it. I'll see you there sometime, Victoria."

"Until then," I said and walked out of her office.

As I was tucking the receipt and her business card into my handbag, Moose was leaning against the side of his truck.

He asked, "What took you so long?"

"I was having a nice conversation with Monica," I admitted.

"So, the M stands for Monica. I really botched that one up, didn't I?"

"You did fine," I said as I patted my grandfather's shoulder. "I think you helped break the ice with your bluster, and when you left, she and I had a nice little conversation."

"What did she say?"

"I'd tell you," I said as I got the receipt out, "but I'm afraid that it's covered under attorney-client privilege now."

"You hired her?" he asked incredulously.

"I did."

I retrieved the receipt and offered it to him. He took it gingerly from me, shook his head when he saw the amount I'd paid, and then handed the paper back to me. "Are you sure you got what you paid for?"

"Are you questioning my judgment?" I asked him.

"What? No, of course not. I'm sure you did what you thought was right. So, was she any help at all?"

"She advised us in a roundabout way that we might have some luck if we go to the BBQ Pit. It's two blocks over and one down."

"You don't have to tell me where it is. Charlie and I go

way back, if the old scoundrel is still running things there."

"Moose, we're not going to have a repeat of what just happened, are we?"

"Victoria, you might be better with lawyers than I am, but I can handle anyone from a fry cook to the head chef if I need to. It doesn't matter what we cook; we all speak the same language. If there's any information here to be had about Howard Lance, I'll get it."

"Well, if nothing else, I admire your confidence," I said with a laugh as we got into the truck and drove over to the BBQ Pit.

Chapter 8

"Charlie, you old horse thief. Don't tell me you're still hanging around this joint after all these years."

"Moose, when did you get out of jail?" he asked my grandfather with a grin.

"They've never been smart enough to catch me," he replied, and the two men started laughing. Their conversation had attracted a great deal of attention from the other patrons there, but as soon as they saw that Charlie was happy about seeing Moose, most of them went back to their meals. The BBQ Pit must have spent every dime they earned on their food, since their decorations appeared to be unchanged from the fifties. It wasn't one of those sleek, retro look places, either. The walls had earned every faded square inch of paint and paper, and the floor was a uniform gray concrete that offered a roadmap of stains and spills from over the years. The place would have been depressing if not for the lively music coming from a jukebox in the corner, and the satisfied smiles of diners all around me. The place just oozed character, and despite my recent meal at The Charming Moose, I felt tempted to try the food there. How had I missed this place, being just half an hour from home? I suppose it was because I spent so much time in our diner that I didn't care much for checking out other places on one of my rare days off, but I was beginning to think that might have been a mistake.

"Come on back to the kitchen," Charlie said. "I want to show you my new smoker."

"You actually cracked open your wallet and bought something new?" Moose asked in genuine surprise.

"No, I swapped for it. I catered a big wedding in Lenoir, and they offered me the smoker in exchange for it. It works like a charm."

"This I've got to see," Moose said as the two men disappeared into the kitchen.

It appeared that, at least for now, I was on my own. I took a seat at the double U serpentine shaped bar and grabbed a menu. Though the restaurant looked old and worn, the menus were spotless, something I appreciated, running The Charming Moose.

A waitress in her forties approached me wearing jeans and a checkered blouse as well as sporting a white starched apron. The nametag that hung from it said, "Josephine."

I pointed to it and said, "Now, there's a name you don't see much these days. I like it."

She grinned. "You're welcome to it, then."

"You could always just go by Jo," I offered.

"That's the one name in the world I hate more than Josephine," she admitted. "What's yours? I might be willing to swap if I like it."

"I'm Victoria," I said as I extended one hand.

"On second thought, I believe I'll keep mine, though you can have my married name for free. I'm done with it, now and forever."

"Did you have a bad breakup?" I asked. That was one thing I loved about being from the South. Most anyone will tell you their life story with the slightest bit of provocation, especially folks who worked in the food service industry.

"The worst. He was bad enough when he was alive, but now the fool has gone and got himself killed, and I don't know what to do about it." As she said it, the tears began, and she put down her order pad and hurried out the front door.

I followed her outside, and found her leaning against a side wall of the building.

"Can I do anything to help?" I asked as I approached her.

She was startled to find me beside her, and quickly dabbed at her eyes with a linen handkerchief. "I'm sorry; I shouldn't have taken off like that. The funniest thing is that I'm not even sure why I'm mourning him. He was a weasel when we were married, and he just got worse after the divorce. So, you tell me why I'm crying for him now that he's gone."

As she spoke, gears started lining up in my head. "You weren't married to Howard Lance by any chance, were you?"

She frowned. "You're not from around here. I know because I never forget a face. How could you possibly know that?"

I could have lied to her right then and there, but I just couldn't bring myself to do it, no matter how bad the circumstances might look to her. "Your ex was killed in my freezer," I said.

Josephine looked at me as though I'd just proclaimed myself the governor of one of the thirteen original colonies. "Lady, if you're joking, I've got to tell you, it's in pretty bad taste."

"My name's Victoria, and I run The Charming Moose," I said.

She looked hard at me, and then said, "I've got nothing to say to you."

"Hang on a second," I said, trying to stop her before she could leave. "I didn't kill him, and neither did anyone else in my family. We're trying to find out who did, though."

"So you decide to set me up, is that it? You knew who I was all along, didn't you? You must think you're pretty clever, tricking me like that."

I was so shocked by the outrageousness of her claim that it took me a second to figure out what to say. "I had no idea Howard Lance even had an ex-wife when you approached me just now, and that's the truth."

"It's a shame that I don't believe you," Josephine said as she headed for the parking lot instead of back into the restaurant.

"Aren't you supposed to be working?" I called out after her as she moved toward an old Honda Civic that had seen better days.

"Tell Charlie I went home sick," she said as she got in

and drove off.

Wow, I'd chided Moose for not being good with people, and I'd just managed to run off someone I'd desperately wanted to talk to. He was going to have a field day with that; there was no doubt in my mind.

When I walked back in, another server, this one a young woman in her twenties with pale blonde bangs and a stick figure, approached me. The name Stacy was embroidered on her apron. "What happened to Jo?" she asked.

"She had to go home. She told me to tell Charlie that she was sick."

"I find that hard to believe," Stacy said. "Was it about Howard again? She's been falling apart ever since she heard the news."

"It was," I admitted. "She seems pretty torn up about what happened to him."

Stacy clearly didn't buy that for a second. "Josephine hated the ground that man walked on, and she wasn't afraid who knew it. She didn't want him, but when the two of us started going out, you'd have thought that I'd taken a shot at her in the parking lot. She started telling folks around town that they'd just about reconciled when I came into the picture, but believe me, nothing could be further from the truth. It wasn't until I started going out with him that she even noticed the man was alive again."

"You were dating Howard Lance?" I asked. This man had some kind of gall, dating a woman who worked with his ex-wife.

"Believe me, he could be smooth when he wanted to be," Stacy said. "It wasn't anything all that serious, but he still didn't deserve what he got."

"You seem to be taking it rather well," I said.

"What do you want me to do, sit at home and cry in my beer? I refuse to shed any crocodile tears for him, but I guarantee you one thing; I'll miss him more than Jo will."

"I thought she liked being called Josephine."

"She does," Stacy answered with a wicked grin. "Can I

get you something?"

"Some sweet tea is all," I said, as tempted as I was by the aromas of pure goodness wafting all around me.

"Are you sure? We make a pretty mean sampler plate here, and it's not really all that much food."

How could I say no? "Tell you what, why don't you just bring me a small side of pulled pork along with that tea?"

"No baked beans or slaw? You can't just have the pork."

I gave up. "Okay. Small sides of pulled pork, baked beans, and slaw. And don't bring me anything else, no matter how much I plead with you."

"I can do that," she said.

While she was in the kitchen getting my order, I had to wonder about the women in Howard Lance's life. His ex-wife seemed genuinely upset that he was dead, the regret written all over her. But was it unhappiness for losing him before they could reconcile, or angst over killing him? Josephine's temper had been volatile enough when we'd spoken, and that kind of passion could easily switch into rage. And what about Stacy? She'd seemed nonchalant enough about Howard, but was she simply distancing herself from the man so soon after his murder as a way of deflecting any suspicion that might come her way? I was still trying to figure it all out when Stacy came back with my plate. If these portions were sides, what must the full-sized plates look like? There was no way I was going to be able to eat all of the food in front of me. I promised myself a fair sampling of each of the offerings, and then I'd leave the rest of it alone. First, I took a sip of tea, knowing that this was the make-or-break point for most restaurants in the South. Made properly, it seemed to ooze out of the glass, heavy with sugar and rich tea flavors, and I wasn't disappointed with this taste. So far, so good. Next, I grabbed a piece of the pulled pork with my fingers and was pleased by the moisture it exuded, though no sauce had been added to it. The piece I'd chosen had a blackened edge with a band of darkness that I knew from experience was a legitimate smoke ring caused by the smoking process infusing the meat. I was expecting something good the second I saw that, but the explosion of flavor in my mouth let me know that this was a treat I wasn't going to miss again. Taking another bite, I marveled at the taste, and then grabbed a fork to sample the slaw and the beans. Baked beans could go either way, I knew from experience, but this batch had never seen the inside of a can. Along with the perfectly cooked beans, I found diced chunks of pickle and barbeque, bathed in a sauce that made the combination melt in my mouth. One taste of the slaw, rich and crisp as a subtle counter to the barbeque, and I knew that my plan to merely sample the plate was now hopeless. As I devoured the meal, I just hoped that I could find it in my heart to keep from ordering seconds.

Stacy stopped by and topped off my tea. "Good, isn't it?"

"It's unbelievable," I admitted as I looked her in the eye. She'd been crying, that was clear, but she'd wiped away her tears and had put on a happy face, so I wasn't about to challenge her about it.

"Are you ready for round two?"

"I couldn't eat another bite," I said, and sadly, it was true.

"You don't want to miss the peach cobbler. It's what we're known for around here."

I almost ordered it, but I couldn't bring myself to do it. I had to have at least one shred of self-discipline, and this had to be where I made my last stand. "Thanks, but no thanks. I'm going to have trouble walking out of here as it is, I ate so much."

"Well, don't fret, there's always next time."

I paid her then and there, told her to keep the change, and asked for my tea to be transferred over to a Styrofoam cup. She brought it back, but there was still no sign of Moose. I figured it might not be a bad idea of taking a run at Stacy, especially since she'd already finished serving me. I knew from experience at the diner with a waitress we'd had to fire long ago that it didn't pay to pick a fight with your server before you got all of your food and drink.

"You look upset," I said. "It's okay to let it out, you know."

"I don't know what you're talking about," she said as she dabbed again at her eyes. "I already told you, Howard and I were just casual."

"Is that really true, Stacy? Because I heard differently." This was a bald-faced lie meant to prod her a little, but it worked far better than I'd expected.

"You are a liar, then!" she shouted at me. "Get out!"

"Hold on," I said, trying to soothe her with my voice. "I didn't mean anything by it."

"Just go!" she demanded again. It must have been loud enough for the men in back to hear. Charlie burst out of the kitchen, with Moose close on his heels.

"What's going on out here?" Charlie asked fiercely.

"She can't talk to me that way, Happy!" Stacy said.

"What did you say to her, Victoria?" Moose asked, clearly concerned about the confrontation I'd started without meaning to. Well, I had meant to get a rise out of the woman, just not one quite so melodramatic.

"I just asked her about Howard Lance," I explained.

Charlie looked at his server. "Is that true?"

"She kept after me about it and wouldn't let go," Stacy said, her voice calmer now.

"You know you aren't supposed to yell at our customers. We've had this talk one too many times."

"What are you going to do, fire me? I can't see you waiting on customers and running the kitchen, too."

"What are you talking about?" he asked as he looked around. "Where's Josephine?"

"Don't ask me. This woman ran her off, too. So, am I fired or what?"

"Just keep it down," Charlie said, and then looked at Moose without saying a word.

"We were just leaving," he said as he took my arm and led me out of the restaurant.

"Do you mind explaining to me again what just happened in there?" Moose asked.

"You're not going to believe it. Howard used to be married to Josephine, and then he started dating Stacy."

"Then it's true? You ran one server off, and so then you decided to go after the other one?"

It was clear that my grandfather had already made up his mind. "Moose, I can't talk to you when you're like this," I said as we got into the truck.

"You don't have any choice, young lady," he said as he drove off. I fully expected my grandfather to head back to Jasper Fork, but to my surprise, he went around the corner, found a parking spot, and then pulled his truck into it and shut off the engine.

"Talk to me," he said, and I decided that being petulant about it wouldn't serve either one of us at the moment. As dispassionately as I could, I told Moose all I'd learned, including my impressions of both women. As I finished, I added, "I still don't think that I did anything wrong."

"Neither do I," Moose answered.

I was about to protest when I realized that my grandfather had just agreed with me. "What did you just say?"

"Given the circumstances, I think you did a fine job in there. Sure, I would have liked to be able to take you back there sometime, but you got the information we were looking for, and that's what matters."

"Thanks. I appreciate that. Were you able to learn anything new while you were back there in the kitchen with Charlie?"

"I've got a great idea I want to run past your husband. We can upgrade our smoked pork barbeque without too much time or money, and I for one think we should do it."

"I meant about the case," I said.

"That was a little bit tougher," he said. "I did find out a few things, but nothing quite as explosive as you did."

"Hey, I'm still eager to hear it."

Moose took a deep breath, and then said, "You already

got most of it. The only thing that Charlie told me that you don't already know is that he's heard around town that Howard left all of his money to one of the two ladies you had confrontations with today. That could be a motive, couldn't it?"

"Sure it could. Did he happen to say how much Howard was worth?"

"No," Moose said, "but a few thousand dollars could mean quite a bit to somebody who is drowning in debt. Who knows if it's even true, though?"

"Agreed, but I've got a hunch that this particular rumor is right on the money."

"Why do you say that? Do you know something that I don't?"

I thought about how hard Monica had pushed me in the direction of the BBQ Pit, and I had to wonder if she weren't telling me the same thing without actually coming out and saying it directly. "He was probably planning on a big score from his extortion. Who knows, maybe one of the ladies misunderstood and thought he had the money already. It's not that big a stretch to see either one of them speeding up their inheritance."

"That's a great theory, but do you have any facts to back it up?" Moose asked.

"No, let's just call it a hunch."

"As long as we don't call it woman's intuition," Moose said.

I laughed. "Don't you believe in that, Moose?" I asked him.

"You're never going to get a straight answer for that question out of me, so you might as well stop asking," he replied. "I think we've done all of the damage we can here. What say we go back to the diner and see if anyone there has heard anything else that might help us?"

"Do you think folks are just going to stop by and volunteer clues?" I asked him.

"Victoria, you know as well as I do that folks love to talk, and the place most of them come to gab is our diner. I'd be amazed if we didn't do more good by hanging around there than gallivanting all over seven counties hunting down clues for ourselves."

"You might be right, but I'm not going to stop trying. The quicker we solve this murder, the better off all of us will be."

Moose nodded, and then a few miles farther down the road, he asked, "So, do you have any favorites yet on our list of suspects?"

"I don't know. I guess it all depends on who you believe. I'm having trouble with Josephine and Stacy here. One is acting as though she's going to miss Howard, and the other is putting on a front that she could care less."

"Both could be true, though, right?"

"Sure it could, Moose. The only problem is that I'd think that the ex-wife wouldn't care as much about the man as the woman he was dating up until he was murdered."

We drove a little more, and then my grandfather asked me, "What about the folks we suspect in Jasper Fork?"

I gave that question a little thought before I said, "I still can't see any of them as a murderer. Bob and Francie could go either way, Cynthia was even shakier, but then again, she always strikes me that way. As for Margie and Hank, I have no idea what their story is. In a lot of ways, I'm more confused than ever."

"Give it time, Victoria. I know that you'll get there."

"I just wish I had the same kind of faith in me as you do," I replied.

"Girl, I've known you your entire life, and if there's one thing that I'm sure of, it's that you'll stick with this until you come up with the right answer. You've always had the stubborn streak of ten bulls."

"Like grandfather, like granddaughter," I answered, which was my usual response when Moose said something like that.

"You can bet your last dollar on that," he said.

Moose's Roasted Chicken

My family loves this meal, and by changing up the veggies every now and then, it can show up more than once on your menu without complaints. Marinating the chicken is optional, and if you're short on time, feel free to skip it. This one's also a cleanup favorite, as all the cooking goes on in a Reynolds Oven Bag.

Ingredients

1 large Reynolds Oven Bag
1 Tablespoon flour, bleached or unbleached (to coat the inside of the bag)

1 teaspoon Italian Seasoning, dried
1 clove garlic, minced
The juice from one lemon (about 3 tablespoons)
2-3 Tablespoons olive oil (I like extra virgin, but plain is fine)

Chicken, quartered and skinned, or three to four chicken breasts
2 cups carrots, peeled, and cut up into finger sized pieces
1 onion, peeled and cut into wedges (I like sweet onions when they're available)
Salt and pepper to taste
3 small new potatoes or equivalent, cut into ½ inch slices

Optional veggies could include:
Bell peppers, green or red
Squash
Etc.

Directions

Preheat the oven to 350 degrees F.

Add the flour and coat the inside of the cooking bag to prevent the bag from exploding.

Add the oil, lemon juice, Italian seasoning, and garlic into the bag and shake it up.

Option 1: Add the chicken pieces now and marinate for 1-4 hours.

Option 2: Add the chicken pieces and toss the bag again, coating the chicken.

Add your vegetables in similar thicknesses to insure even cooking.

Tie the bag, and then make 4-6 horizontal slashes to allow steam to escape.

Place in a baking dish and cook for 1 hour, or until the chicken has reached 175 degrees F.

Let rest 10 minutes (if you can wait that long) and serve.

Rice or mashed potatoes make a nice side dish with this meal, especially if you skip the potatoes in the meal itself.

Chapter 9

As soon as we walked back into our diner, Ellen Hightower cornered me. Her shift had been over twenty minutes by my calculation, and she looked intent on talking to me. "I'm so glad you're here," she said. "I waited just about as long as I could."

"What's going on?" I asked. She got off at two every day to be there when her kids got off the school bus, and finding her at The Charming Moose after hours was nearly unheard of.

"I heard something that might be important," she said as she lowered her voice, "but I don't want to talk about it in here."

I nodded, and then I turned to my grandfather. "Moose, I need you to cover for me for a few minutes." My grandfather was always willing to lend a hand, whether it was waiting tables and working the register or helping out in back at the grill.

"What can I do?"

I looked around and said, "Take care of the tables, the register, and if you get a chance, clean a few tables."

He grabbed an apron from behind the counter and put it on. "You've got it."

"Come on," I told Ellen as I walked out the front door.

Once we were in the parking lot, I asked, "Now, what's so important?"

"You're looking for Hank Brewer and Margie Collins, is that right?"

How had she heard about our search for our missing suspects? Greg must have told her, or perhaps she'd overheard Moose and me when we'd been talking about our murder investigation. Either way, it appeared that we might be about to get a break. "We are. Did you hear something about them? Where are they?"

"I don't know exactly, but I heard that they were together," Ellen said.

"Where did you pick that up?"

She hesitated, and then looked down at the ground. "I'd really rather not say. I don't want anyone in town thinking that I'm some kind of gossip."

"I can respect that," I said, "and I promise not to reveal my source, but it could be a big help to know."

She still looked anguished about the prospect of talking. "Victoria, I can't ask you to keep this from your family. If I tell you, I know that you'll tell Greg and Moose, and I can't afford to lose this job. I have a family to take care of."

I took her hands in mine as I said, "Ellen, unless I catch you with your hand in the till or doing something outrageous to one of our customers, your job is safe here. I'm the one in charge here, remember? You can trust me."

"So, you won't tell anybody?"

"If there's any way to keep from it, I won't breathe a word to another soul," I promised. It would be a hard one to keep, especially with Moose, but I was bound and determined to do it. My family was important, but my word, and my honor, were even more significant to me. I'd had it drilled into me from an early age that without trust, nothing else mattered.

"Okay. I heard Karen Morgan telling the Reverend Mercer something about them being together, but when I got closer, Karen clammed up. I know it's not much, Victoria, but it's the best I can do."

"You did great," I said. "And don't worry about me. I won't tell anyone where I got the information."

"Are you going to go talk to one of them?" she asked.

"Well, it sounds as though the good reverend was just the recipient of the news. Karen's the one I need to chat with."

"Thanks for keeping my secret," she said, the relief clear on her face.

"You've got it. Now hurry home. You don't want to miss your kids."

"It's what I live for," she said with a huge grin, and then softened it. "Not that I don't love coming here to work every day."

"Ellen, if your family isn't more important to you than your job, I'd probably have to fire you. I don't want anyone working here who doesn't have a heart, too."

"Thanks," she said as she got into her ratty old station wagon and drove toward home.

I thought about popping in and telling Moose what Ellen had just shared with me, but if I did that, I knew that he'd want to tag along, and that would leave us shorthanded at the diner.

Just this once, I decided to go talk to Karen on my own.

She was at her place in the records room when I walked in, digging into one of the dusty volumes there. I glanced at the spine quickly, just to make sure that it wasn't 1959. It wasn't, but I'd hoped for it, if only for a flash.

She looked up after putting a finger in the volume, to hold her place most likely, and smiled ruefully at me. "I'm sorry to report that there's still no sign of the ledger," she said.

"That's not why I'm here," I said.

Karen looked surprised by the statement, but she took a call slip and put it in the volume before closing it. "What can I do for you, then?"

"I want to know where Hank and Margie are, and don't bother trying to deny that you have a pretty good idea. I know you've got more information about this than you're letting on."

"What gives you that idea?" she asked, the friendly smile now gone.

"Let's just say that I have a sound source."

Karen looked mad enough to spit. "That's the last time I try to get some advice from that no-good preacher. I don't care what he told you. I shared something with him in confidence, and if he can't keep a secret, what good is he?

Folks are going to hear about this around town, believe me."

Oh, no. I couldn't let that stand. The man had done nothing worth having his reputation shredded. "I didn't hear anything from him."

"Why should I believe you?" Karen asked.

"You know how I feel about lying. The reverend is innocent."

That seemed to mollify her a little. "If he didn't tell you, then, who did?"

"Karen, it's no secret the two of you were talking earlier at the diner. How many people were sitting close enough to overhear your conversation? Can you even count them all?"

I was hoping the place had been fairly full, since I needed my customers as a screen for Ellen.

"There were probably close to a dozen," she said reluctantly.

"There you go, then. It doesn't matter who told me about it. I want to know the truth. Where are they now?"

"I don't know," Karen said, "and that's the truth."

"Then what were you telling him?" Had Ellen been wrong after all? No, I doubted that, else why would Karen have reacted so strongly to my questions?

"I might not know where they are at the moment, but I have a real suspicion that they're together," she finally acknowledged.

"What makes you say that?" I asked.

She took a few seconds to think about replying before she finally spoke. "The two of them have been secretly dating for months," she said. "It started out innocent enough, and I'm sure that Margie was just trying to comfort Hank, but lately it's been leading to something else."

"How did you find out, when everyone else around here was in the dark about their relationship?"

She shrugged. "I don't know if you're aware of it, but I have insomnia. Most nights I just get four or five hours of sleep, and I feel trapped at the apartment sometimes, so I walk."

This was indeed news. "Where do you go?"

"I just let my mind wander and see where the nights lead me."

"Aren't you afraid?" I asked. I couldn't imagine doing it myself. Our town was generally safe enough, but that didn't mean that I was in any hurry to tempt fate.

"I carry a few things with me just in case, but I've never felt threatened in the least," she admitted. "One night last month I was walking down Margie's street, and I saw a figure in the shadows slip around her house. It all looked fairly sinister, and I was about to report it to Sheriff Croft when I saw that it was Hank. He slunk to his car, and then I saw him wave in the faint light from the streetlight down the block. Margie's porch light flickered on and then off again quickly, and I knew that she was giving him some sort of signal."

"And you didn't tell anybody about it then?" I asked.

"I'm not a gossip, and if the two of them wanted to sneak around like teenagers, I figured they had their reasons."

"But you know more than that, don't you?" I asked.

Karen looked a little embarrassed as she admitted, "I happened to mention what I'd seen to Margie, and she broke down and told me all about it. I didn't think anything more of it, and then I heard about the murder in your freezer. Word around town was that they were both suspects, so I had to tell someone and get another opinion. I still didn't want to say anything until I was sure that it was important. That's why I asked the reverend to meet me at the diner. I figured he'd be able to tell me what to do. I never dreamed someone there would repeat to you what I'd said."

"It's a small town," I said, intent on not saying anything that might lead her to suspect Ellen as my informant. "So, what did he say when you asked him about it?"

"He advised me to tell the sheriff, and I asked him to keep the source a secret."

"That sounds like a solid plan to me," I said.

"It's kind of too late for that, though, isn't it?"

"What do you mean?"

Karen frowned as she explained, "Well, I just told you, didn't I? How long is it going to be before everyone else in Jasper Fork knows?"

"If they do, they won't hear it from me," I said firmly. "This won't be the first secret I've kept from the town."

"Really? Like what?"

I smiled as I shook a finger at her. "Nice try, but I'm not falling for it. Go tell the sheriff, and forget you said a word about any of it to me."

"Really?" she asked as she came around the counter and hugged me. "I can't tell you how relieved I am just telling someone else what I know."

"Don't get too comfortable with that feeling yet," I said. "You need to tell Sheriff Croft, and I mean right now. It might impact how he carries on his investigation."

Karen looked at me oddly. "Do you really think that one of them might have had something to do with the murder?"

"I don't know, but it really doesn't matter what I think. The sheriff needs all of the information he can get if he's going to have any luck solving this case."

"How about you?" Karen asked.

"How about me what?"

"Don't try to duck the question, Victoria. I know that you and Moose have been trying to solve this murder yourselves."

I wasn't all that thrilled that folks knew what we were up to, but honestly, it hadn't been that hard to figure out. I'd wanted to approach things subtly, but my grandfather didn't have that particular trick in his bag. "We're doing a little digging on the side," I admitted. "But who wouldn't? Our family's good name is at risk here."

"I understand completely, you don't have to explain anything to me. Thanks for listening," she said with honest gratitude.

"You can always talk to me," I said as I left the records

room.

I was nearly out the door when I heard a voice calling me from the opposite hallway. It was Sheriff Croft, and I wasn't all that keen to talk to him, but what choice did I have? I turned around and offered him my best smile. "Hello, Sheriff. How are you?"

"Overworked and underpaid," he said, something that was his go-to response most days. "What were you doing in there just now, if I might ask?" he asked as he pointed to the records room.

"I needed to talk to Karen about something," I said. "Well, I'd love to hang around and chat, but I've got a diner to run."

"Not so fast," he said. "Was it about the murder?"

That stopped me in my tracks. "What's not these days? It seems to be all that anybody in Jasper Fork is thinking about these days."

"Victoria, that's not really an answer, now, is it?"

I decided it was time to make an executive decision. "Talk to Karen. You'll be glad that you did."

He looked troubled by my response. "What do you know that I don't?"

I bit back a dozen different sarcastic answers that instantly sprang to mind. This obviously wasn't the time for my wit. "She has something to share with you, and you're better off hearing it directly from her than second-hand."

"I hate being the last to know something," he admitted.

"Don't feel bad. I stumbled onto this purely by accident, and the second I heard what she had to say, I practically begged her to go to you with it."

He clearly looked as though he didn't believe it, and then his cell phone rang. "This is the sheriff. Yes. Fine. I'll be right there." After he hung up, he smiled at me softly. "That's a point for you."

"Was it Karen?" I hoped that she'd followed my advice, but I wasn't counting on it.

"It was," he said. "She needs to talk to me."

"Then I'd go before she changes her mind," I said.

"I'll do just that. And Victoria?"

"Yes," I answered, hoping that our question and answer session was over, at least for the moment.

"Thank you," he said.

"Glad to help," I replied, and then I got out of there while things were still on a good note between us.

Back at the diner, Moose opened the door for me when I walked back in. Four tables were filled, each in varying stages of dining, along with a few folks at the counter, and all of the tables were clean. Moose could be a real machine when he put his mind to it.

"Where have you been?" he asked, clearly exasperated by my absence.

"I was talking to Ellen outside, remember?"

"After she left, I saw you set off on foot toward the courthouse. What did you do, decide to take a little stroll?"

"Are you spying on me, Moose?" I asked, trying to make light of it.

"When there's a murderer loose in our town, you'd better believe that I am," he said. "Victoria, you can't take any chances, especially not now."

"Do I need to remind you yet again that I'm a grown woman? I appreciate your concern, but I can take care of myself."

"In a debate, there's no doubt in my mind, but in a knife fight, I'd have to put my money on the bad guy."

"Then you'd lose," I said. It was time to confess, at least part of what I knew. "I just went to the records room."

"What did you have to say to Karen? Did she find that missing ledger, or the logbook?"

"Neither one, as far as I know," I said, wondering how I was going to keep my real motivation for visiting the clerk from my grandfather. I loved my family without reservation, but my word was my word.

"Then why were you there?"

I should have known that he wasn't about to let it go. "Because I heard a rumor that I wanted to check out."

"What did you hear that I didn't? Did something happen at the BBQ Pit that you didn't share with me?"

"Moose, I told you everything."

He looked at me cagily. "Then, or now?"

"Then," I admitted. "Listen, I gave my word to keep what I heard, and where I heard it, to myself. Do me a favor and don't start guessing, or pushing me about any of it. You had a hand in putting this honor code into my DNA, so I'd appreciate it if you didn't try to make me break it, okay?"

"I understand completely," he said, and then he hugged me gently.

"What was that for?"

"Being my granddaughter isn't enough?" he asked.

"I guess it will have to do," I said with a grin. "Anyway, I have a hunch that you'll hear about it soon enough."

"Just one question, then," he asked. "Does it play any part in our investigation?"

"It does," I admitted, though not without some angst about acknowledging even that much.

"Was giving your word of honor the only way you were able to acquire the new information?" he asked me sternly.

"It was," I said. I'd learned long ago that with Moose, sometimes it was best to supply as little as I could in the form of answers to his direct questions.

"Then I trust you completely," he said, and handed me his apron. "Unless you have any new leads to follow, it might be a good time for you to take over."

"What are you going to be doing?" I asked.

"Truthfully, all of this running around has worn me out a little. I thought I might go home and grab a little nap while I could."

"Are you feeling okay?" I asked him. Sometimes I forgot just how old my grandfather really was, and I knew that while he hadn't missed a beat with most things since he'd gotten older, he didn't seem to be able to draw on the necessary reserves when he needed it like he used to. I reminded myself yet again that I was lucky to have him still with me, and I made a promise not to take my time with him for granted, no matter how much he projected the idea that he was going to live forever.

"Don't worry about me, child. I'm as strong as my namesake," he said as he patted his chest.

"Well, even a moose needs a nap every now and then," I said. "I'll let you know if anything comes up in the meantime. Moose, thanks for understanding."

"I didn't really have much choice, now, did I?" he asked. "You made a good point, and probably the only one that would have shut me up. Honor is extremely important to this family, and I'm glad to see that you're keeping it strong for another generation. You know, it might not be a bad idea to add another branch to the family tree. Victoria, we could all really use a baby around here. Somebody's going to need to keep this joint open after we're all gone."

I grinned at him, having grown quite adept at dodging that particular question. "That's a worry for another day."

"Just don't wait too long," he said.

"Have a good nap, Moose."

"I get it," he said with a wink. "But don't think this discussion is over."

"I wouldn't dream of it," I said.

Greg came out a few seconds later and asked me, "What was that all about?"

"Moose was fishing around for a grandchild again," I said.

Greg surprised me by wrapping me up in his arms, though customers were all around us. He normally wasn't all that big on public displays of affection, and it always pleasantly surprised me when he indulged in a little. "What did you tell him?"

"That we weren't in any hurry," I replied. "Do you still feel that way, too?"

"I'm happy just enjoying the chance to be with you,"

Greg said.

"That is the perfect answer," I answered, and then grabbed a quick kiss.

"Maybe someday, though," Greg said, smiling as his words trailed off.

"Maybe someday," I repeated, answering him with a grin of my very own.

Chapter 10

"Hey, Stranger," Rebecca Davis said as she came into the diner a few minutes later. She was wearing a nice black dress that showed off her figure without flaunting it. "Did you miss me?" Rebecca was close enough in appearance to me to be my sister. We wore the same size to the point where we could even share a wardrobe, but that was where it ended. I couldn't imagine that she'd ever want to borrow a pair of my jeans, or my limited selection of plain shirts and blouses, but I couldn't say the same thing about me. Rebecca tended to choose suits and dresses that were more appropriate for her profession, and I'd dipped into her closet for a special occasion more than once. We'd grown up together in Jasper Fork, and though we'd gone to college together and had been roommates all four years, I'd come back home to marry Greg when I graduated, while she went on to law school. I knew that a break like that was enough to doom more than one relationship, but we'd stayed solid through her years away, and when she'd come back home to hang her shingle, I'd reveled in getting her back in my daily life.

"You have no idea," I said as I hugged her. I hadn't realized just how much I'd missed her support until she was back.

"What happened, Vee?" she asked. Rebecca was the only person in the world—including my family, even my husband—to call me that. I called her Becka, but not all that often now that she was an attorney.

"Somebody was murdered in our deep freezer while you were gone," I said softly. There were a few folks eating, and I didn't want to add any to the gossip already tearing around town about us.

"If I didn't know any better, I'd say that you were kidding, but I know that look on your face. That's just terrible. Was it someone I knew?"

"I doubt it. A man named Howard Lance came by the diner a few nights ago claiming that he owned the land The Charming Moose sits on. He had a legal document and everything."

"And I wasn't here to help you," she said, a look of despair coming onto her face. "Why didn't you call me?"

"There wasn't anything you could do about it," I explained. "And besides, Moose brought in a big gun as soon as he heard about it."

"I bet he hit the roof," Rebecca said as a slight smile appeared on her face, and then vanished just as quickly.

"He wasn't happy," I admitted, "and even less after Holly Dixon left here."

"He called Judge Dixon for legal advice?" she asked, clearly incredulous about that particular development. "She's as tough as they come. How did Moose manage to get that particular string to pull?"

"According to him, they've been friends for a long time."

"But you don't buy it, do you?" Rebecca asked.

"It's not me as much as my grandmother," I said. "Martha left the diner pretty quickly when the judge came by to examine the document."

"Let me see it," she said, digging a pair of reading glasses out of her stylish purse.

"No worries. We already found out that it was just an extortion attempt that had no real foundation. Howard Lance was trying to get a few quick scores before we found out, but evidently somebody didn't take too kindly to being extorted."

"I can't imagine anyone liking it," she said. "If it was a legal document, you should see who drafted it. There might be something valuable there."

"Moose and I are one step ahead of you. We tracked down an attorney in Laurel Landing, and she basically confirmed that she'd done it without giving us anything about Howard."

"What's his name?" Rebecca asked. "I might know

him."

"It was a she, actually. Have you ever heard of Monica Ingram?"

Rebecca nodded. "She's supposed to be good. In fact, I'm amazed that you got anything out of her at all."

"Believe me, she was pretty cagey about it all, but it was clear that she honestly wanted to give us a hand. You should look her up, Rebecca. I have a hunch that the two of you would get along famously."

"Thanks, but I have enough acquaintances who are attorneys now. I cannot believe that I wasn't here when you needed me."

"Don't beat yourself up. You deserved some time away."

"I can't help regretting it right now, though. At least you're out of it."

I looked down at the floor for a few seconds, and then just kind of shrugged.

Rebecca didn't miss a beat. "Are you trying to tell me that you're not out of it?"

"He was murdered in our restaurant, Becka," I said. "And it's not like we all didn't have motives."

She nodded. "I get it. Every one of you are suspects. I bet Sheriff Croft is just loving that."

"Actually, he's given Moose and me quite a bit of latitude digging around."

That caught her completely off guard. "Hang on one second, young lady. Are you telling me that your grandfather is working with you to track down a killer?"

"It's not as bad as it sounds," I said. "It turns out that we make a pretty good team."

"Will wonders never cease. What does your better half say about that?"

"Honestly, I think he's just happy he gets to stay in the kitchen," I admitted.

She shook her head, and then said, "I'll say this for you. You really know how to overwhelm a gal. Is there any chance I might get a piece of pie so I can have a little time to catch my breath?"

"You've got it," I said. "Any preferences?"

"As long as someone here made it, I'm pretty sure that I'll be happy with it."

I grabbed her a slice of peach pie from the kitchen, and as I did, Greg said, "Tell Rebecca I'm glad she's back home."

"For my sake or hers?" I asked as I got a cup and saucer for her.

"For everyone's," he said. "Have you brought her up to speed yet about the murder?"

"I'm working on it."

"Carry on, then," he said as he waved his spatula in the air. There weren't many things my husband wouldn't share if he had to, but the two things I knew for sure were his spatula and me. I never had the nerve to ask his order of preference, mostly just content to be in the top two.

I slid the pie in front of her, and then grabbed one of our coffee pots and filled one of our mugs. She took a nice-sized bite of pie, seemed to let it linger a moment, and then swallowed it, chasing the pie with a healthy gulp of coffee. "There. That's better."

"Than what?" I asked with a grin.

"Than the moment just before there was pie," she said, answering with a smile of her own. "So, who all is on your suspect list?"

I started to tell her, but she held up a hand. "Hang on. I assume that you're sharing this information with the sheriff, is that correct?"

I thought about what Moose and I had learned so far, and nodded. "So far we have," I said.

"That's fine, then; just don't tell me anything you don't want him to know. I'm a sworn officer of the court, you know, and I have to take it seriously. You have a great deal more latitude than I do in what you and your grandfather are doing."

"Does that mean that you can't be my partner in crime, too?" I asked with a laugh.

"Not like the old days," she answered. "Besides, the more I think about it, it might not be a bad idea to keep me in the dark. That way, when the sheriff gets around to arresting the two of you for obstruction of justice, I'll be able to take the case with a clean conscience. Is that all right with you?"

"You'd better believe it. I'm counting on it," I said.

We chatted a little more, and after Rebecca finished her pie and coffee, she said, "I've got to get home and get into some comfortable clothes. What do I owe you for the coffee and pie?"

"It's on the house," I replied.

She didn't agree, though. "Victoria, you know that I always pay my way."

"So do I," I answered, just as stubbornly. "If you'd like, think of it as your retainer for keeping me out of jail."

"I doubt I can do that, but the very least I can do is get you out once you've been arrested. Is that good enough?"

"It sounds good to me," I said.

I was about to say something else when Moose walked in, looking even more distracted than was normal for him. "There you are," he said when he spotted me. "Let's go."

I stood my ground. "Look, Moose. Rebecca's back."

He glanced in her direction, and then shot her a brief grin. "Hey, Counselor. I'd tell you that you look lovely as usual, but I'm sure enough men say the exact same thing to make it a weak compliment."

"You'd be surprised by how little I hear it," she said.

"Then shame on the men of North Carolina and beyond for not recognizing what a treasure they have in you."

"Moose, you are one charming man. This diner is well named."

He shrugged, but it was clear that he liked the compliment from such a lovely woman.

"Be that as it may, I'm afraid that Victoria and I have an errand to run."

"Are you two going to keep investigating?" she asked with the hint of a smile.

"You've been here long enough for Victoria to fill you in?" he asked.

"Mostly I'm keeping out of it."

"So she can get us out of jail if we need busting out," I told my grandfather.

"It's always important to have a contingency plan," he said, and then he looked at me again. "Victoria, are you coming, or do I have to do this all by myself?"

"Hold your horses. I'm ready and willing, but who's going to watch the front while we're gone?" It was just after three, the twilight zone when Ellen was already gone, but Jenny wasn't there yet.

"Your reinforcements will be here in a second."

The front door opened, and I was surprised to see Martha come in. "Are you my relief?" I asked her. "I thought you retired for good."

"What can I say? Your grandfather can be very persuasive when he sets his mind to it."

I kissed her cheek in thanks, and then turned back to Rebecca. "Can we finish catching up later?"

"About everything but the case," she said firmly.

"Don't worry. I was talking about your little adventure. Did you happen to have any love, romance, or intrigue while you were away?"

"Not that you'd notice," she said. "However, there was one attorney from Hickory who has potential."

"You ladies can gab all you want to later about the lucky guy," Moose said. "I mean it, Victoria. I'm going, and I mean right now."

"I'm right behind you," I said. "Do I have time to kiss my husband good bye?"

"Don't worry, I'll personally take care of that for you," Rebecca said with a wicked grin.

"Thanks, but that's one job I'm not about to delegate." I could tell that Moose wasn't happy about this new delay, but that was just tough. Besides, there was no way that Martha was going to let him leave the diner without me.

"Bye," I said as I kissed Greg quickly.

"See you later," he said, intent on filling three orders at the same time. I didn't envy him when things got busy in the kitchen, but he felt the same way when I had a stack of customers waiting to pay their bills during our busiest times. Our division of labor worked out just fine as far as both of us were concerned.

Once Moose and I were out in the parking lot, I asked my grandfather, "What was the big hurry? Is it really that urgent?"

"I don't know," he said with the hint of a smile. "I just thought you might like a look into Howard Lance's apartment in Laurel Landing."

"You know I do, but how did you manage that?"

His grin was out in full force now. "Victoria, I've been alive enough decades to have favors due all over our part of the state, and beyond as well. I found out where Lance was staying, and I managed to get us a quick peek inside if we hurry."

"Do you know if Sheriff Croft has searched the place yet?" I didn't want to get into any trouble that I could avoid, and going to Lance's place before our sheriff made it would be bad on so many levels.

"He's come and gone, and the place is going to be packed up by midnight. I volunteered to do it for the apartment owner. That way, it's a win for everyone. He gets the place cleaned up, and we get to search for clues. You can tell me now how impressed you are with my resourcefulness."

"You know I am," I said as I hugged him before we got into his truck.

It appeared that we were getting a second wind in our investigation. I just hoped we found more than we had so far.

"Moose, there's absolutely nothing here that's going to help us," I said after we'd searched and sorted everything in Howard Lance's apartment. Moose's friend, Duke, the man who owned the place, had provided us with boxes for trash and Goodwill, so at least we'd accomplished something during our hunt.

"I'm sorry," Moose said as he closed up the last box. "I thought for sure we'd find something here."

"The sheriff must have been more thorough than we'd thought."

"Actually, our sheriff is the one who did the search," an older man said as he joined us. "Moose, how are you, you old rascal?"

"Better than most guys our age, Duke," Moose said.

"Did you have any luck?" he asked after Moose introduced me to him.

"Not a bit of it. I've got to tell you, though, I'm surprised Sheriff Croft let someone else search for clues here, even if it is out of his jurisdiction."

"They searched it together," Duke said. "I tried to give them a little advice, but when they both threw me out, I decided to be someplace else quick, if you know what I mean." He looked around the living room, and shook his head in disgust. "It's bad enough that I've had number four empty for five months, now I have to get this one ready to rent again, too. I thought I was buying a slice of retirement when I dropped a load on this place, but all I guaranteed myself was more work."

"We appreciate the chance to look, anyway," Moose said as he started out the door with the last box. We had them sorted and stacked in front of the apartment, and my grandfather shook his friend's hand one last time. "Come by the diner and I'll buy you a cup of coffee sometime," Moose said.

"From what I hear, you're never there anymore."

"Don't worry. I'll make good on it, and I hardly ever leave the place," I said.

"You're gone right now, though, aren't you?" Duke asked with a grin.

"I'll write you an IOU," Moose said, and did just that.

"Present it to the first person who works for us you see, and you'll get your java."

"Where are you going?" Duke said as we took a few steps toward the truck.

My grandfather glanced at his watch. "I can hang around a little bit if you're lonely, but we both have to get back to work."

"I don't want conversation, you old goat," Duke said. "I just thought you'd like to see Lance's storage locker."

"Did you show this to the two sheriffs?" I asked as Duke led us to the back of the building.

"I tried to, but they ran me off before I had a chance. I figured somebody might like to take a peek, though."

Duke opened a side door, and just inside we found a large metal cage with a keyed lock on it. Inside were a dozen storage lockers, each one no bigger than a coffin, but there was still plenty of room to hide something important inside.

"Which one was Lance's?" Moose asked as we all stepped inside.

"He had number nine," Duke said. "I already took care of the lock, but don't worry about cleaning this out. I'll get to it before I make that haul to charity. Now, I'll get out of your way, since there's barely enough room to turn around in there with the two of you. You don't have to stop by when you leave. Just slam the door; it will lock on its own."

"Thanks again," Moose said, and I noticed that he waited until his friend was out the door before he moved to Howard Lance's locker.

"What's the matter, don't you trust him?" I asked softly.

"Oh, I trust him just fine. It's just the seven people he'll tell after that I can't vouch for. The man loves to chat, in case you hadn't noticed."

"Got it." All of the other lockers inside the cage had locks on them. I watched as Moose opened Howard Lance's locker. Inside were several things that might be of interest to a flea market or a yard sale, but I was afraid that it was just more of the same as what we'd found inside.

"Well, that was a waste," Moose said as he closed the locker back.

"How could we know that, though?" I asked. Then, something caught my eye. "Moose, Duke said that number four was empty, too, right?"

"That's right," Moose said.

The only problem was that there was a lock on the storage area, just like the ones on the other, occupied units. I tugged on the lock on a whim, and to my surprise, it came open in my hand. "What's this mean, do you suppose?"

"I'm guessing that Duke never got around to cleaning this one out, either."

"Maybe," I said, and then I pulled the lock all of the way off and opened the door. The first thing I found was the ledger book for 1959 from our records department, and the second was the sign-in book that we'd looked for in vain.

Chapter 11

"I wouldn't do that if I were you," Moose said as I reached for the book.

"Why not? We're the ones who found it, fair and square."

"Go ahead then if you're determined to do it, but think about how Sheriff Croft is going to feel when he finds out that we uncovered a pair of clues when he hadn't had any luck at all."

"Do you think it's better to grab these quietly, or should we call him up just to rub his nose in it?" I asked.

"We're not rubbing his nose into anything. Call him, Victoria, and let him make the decision. After all, that's why he makes the big bucks, right?"

I dialed the sheriff's number, hoping that it would go to voice mail so I wouldn't have to deal with him directly, but it was just my luck; he picked up on the second ring. "Sheriff, Moose and I just found something that you're going to want to see."

"What's that?" he asked, the interest evident in his voice.

"We just finished searching Howard Lance's place," I said.

Before I could give him any more details, he said, "I doubt that. We went through the place pretty thoroughly ourselves."

"How about the storage locker?" I asked, trying my very best not to sound smug as I said it. The last thing I wanted to do was make the sheriff angry.

"What storage locker? Duke didn't say a word about there even being one."

"He told us that he tried to tell you both, but you and the other sheriff wouldn't listen to him."

There was a long silence, and then the sheriff said, "It

was Harley's investigation. He just let me tag along during the search as a favor. I thought it would be a good idea to hear what Duke had to say, but Harley's like that sometimes. He was bent on digging on his own. What did you find?"

"Actually, there was nothing in his unit," I said.

"Then why the dramatic lead-up to all of this, Victoria?"

"Well, on our way out, we noticed that one of the other locks was loose, so naturally we checked it out."

I could hear the impatience growing in his voice. "Are you going to tell me what you found, or do I have to beg for the information?"

"No, sir," I said. "Evidently Howard stashed some things in the empty locker, knowing that no tenant lived there. We discovered the missing registry for 1959, and also the sign-in log for the records room."

"Was there anything else there?" he asked. I now had his full attention; there was no doubt about that.

"Moose thought it might be more prudent if we called you first and got your permission to search before we dug any deeper," I said as I stuck my tongue out at my grandfather.

My grandfather chuckled softly, but didn't make a return expression of any kind.

"Do you have gloves?" the sheriff asked me.

"I've got some gardening gloves at home, but I never use them."

"I meant with you," Sheriff Croft said.

"Gloves," I said softly to my grandfather as I put my hand over the phone.

Moose looked around and came across an old pair on a workbench outside of the cage. "Tell him I just found some," my grandfather said.

I was about to when the sheriff said, "I heard him. Does your cell phone take pictures that you can send?"

"It does," I answered.

"Take a shot of the locker before Moose does another thing, and then send it to me."

That was pretty clever of him, and it was something I hadn't thought to do. "I won't be able to talk while I'm doing it. Give me a call after you've seen the photograph."

"I will, but remember, don't touch a thing."

"You don't have to tell me twice," I said, and then I got a little satisfaction hanging up on the man.

I took a couple of shots of the open locker until I had one I was satisfied with, and then texted it to the sheriff.

"What do we do now?" Moose asked.

"We wait for his answer."

Two minutes later, my phone rang.

"Did they turn out okay?" I asked after seeing that it was the sheriff calling me back.

"Perfect. Now, have Moose take out each book and set it aside. If there's an empty box around there, that would be perfect, but a blanket or towel would do, too."

"How about both?" I asked as I spotted an old sheet in one corner of the room, sitting inside an empty box.

"Perfect," he said. "Have Moose move the books, and then send me another photo of the locker."

I'd been holding the phone out so that my grandfather could hear as well, and he did as he was instructed.

I told Sheriff Croft, "Consider it done. You'll get the shot in a second."

As we waited for the sheriff to call me back, I looked at Moose and said, "This is overkill, isn't it? We've already established that the books were in the locker."

"Just let him do his job, Victoria," Moose said. "He's probably putting his tail on the line even letting us do this, so I'm willing to cooperate in just about any way that he wants us to."

My phone rang again. The sheriff said that he was satisfied with the shots, and then he instructed, "Have Moose pull the rest of the contents out, one at a time, and tell me what you find as he does it."

We did as we were told, but we'd just found the sum total of everything of interest in that locker, at least as far as

Howard Lance was concerned.

"The rest of it's a wash," I told the sheriff as I surveyed the contents we'd pulled out one at a time. In that locker, the things we'd checked hadn't taken up a great deal of room, but spread out on the floor, we barely had room to walk. There were old tools there, a stack of ancient magazines, a collection of paints and brushes that had seen better days, a few loose leaf notebooks that appeared to be empty, and an old drop cloth that was stained with a variety of spilled paints over the years.

"Now, take a photo of everything and send it to me," he instructed, "and then find another box and bring it all back with you. You two did good calling me, Victoria. Thank you."

"It's Moose you should be thanking," I said. "He's the one who thought to do it."

"Well then, tell him that I appreciate it. I expect you both to come straight back to Jasper Fork right now so I can examine the contents myself."

"We're on our way," I assured the sheriff as Moose put the last of it in another box he'd scrounged up in one corner. It was clear from the presence of so many cartons that Duke was prepared for folks to move in and out on him, if the abundance of empty boxes was any indication.

"What did he have to say before you hung up?" Moose asked.

"He wants it all in his office as quickly as we can get it to him," I said.

"I don't blame him a bit. I doubt any of it will do him any good, though. Grab the box with the books, will you? I'll get the rest."

"Okay," I said. "Why do you think it's useless?" I asked as we left the building.

"It's nice to confirm that Howard took the books, but we already knew that he was scamming all of us. As for the rest of it, I doubt any of it was anything but camouflage."

"I hate not making more progress," I said as we stowed

the boxes in the bed of his truck and headed back home.

"How were we supposed to know that we'd just hit another dead end before we came here looking for clues?" Moose asked.

"I'm just getting a little frustrated by our lack of progress," I admitted.

"I know exactly how you feel, but we'll just have to take it in stride and keep digging," my grandfather answered.

"Any idea where we should look next?" I asked.

"No, but we've got a long ride home to think about it."

Unfortunately, we weren't able to come with anything new along the way. We'd get back to the diner in time to close up for the night, and I had no idea what the next day would bring, but I hoped that it was one step closer to finding the killer.

Chapter 12

Greg and I had finished closing the diner, and we were back home not ten minutes when there was a knock at the front door.

"Are you expecting anybody?" Greg asked me as he went to answer it.

"No, how about you?"

"Not so much, and unless it's someone with a great big check with our names on it, I'm sending them away. After what's been happening lately, I just want to hang around here and relax."

Greg came back thirty seconds later with a puzzled expression on his face. "Victoria, it's for you."

"You didn't invite them in?" I asked my husband, normally a very polite man.

"I tried, but she wouldn't leave the porch."

"So you left someone standing out there alone in the dark? At least turn the porch light on."

"Just go talk to her, okay?"

I looked at my husband and frowned. "At least tell me who it is so I'm not going out there blind."

"It's Francie Humphries."

I stopped before I got to the door. "Greg, she's on my list of suspects. There is no way I'm going out there."

"Sorry, I didn't even think of that. Don't worry, I'll handle it."

I had second thoughts about having Greg do my dirty work. What if she did something to him, and I'd been the one to send him out there? "That's okay. I'll talk to her."

"No, you're right. This is crazy. If she wants to talk to you, she can do it out in the open in broad daylight."

I couldn't stop him from going outside, but that didn't mean that I wasn't going to follow him.

"Where is she?" I asked as I looked around our porch and yard.

"She was here a second ago," Greg said, and then louder, he called out, "Francie? We're right here. It's okay. Come on out."

There was no reply.

"What do we do now?" Greg asked.

"I don't know about you, but I'm not going to go out searching the streets looking for her. If she wants to talk to me, she can call, or better yet, come by the diner when we're open. Come on back inside; it's freezing out here."

Greg followed me back in, rubbing his hands together. "The temperature's really falling. How about a fire?"

"That sounds wonderful."

He got out the matches as he said, "Coming right up. I love having a stack of kindling waiting for us." As Greg lit the fire, our home phone rang.

"Hello?" I asked.

"Why wouldn't you come out?" Francie asked plaintively.

"Why did you take off all of a sudden like that?" I countered.

"A car drove by, and I was afraid that it was someone out looking for me."

"Francie, why are you acting so paranoid?" I asked, even though what I should have asked was why she was being even more paranoid than was usual for her. "Do you know something that we don't?"

She paused, and then said, "Honestly? I'm not sure."

"What does that mean?" I asked. There was a hitch in Francie's breathing as she spoke, and I wondered if she was having some kind of panic attack.

"It's too complicated to discuss over the phone," she said.

"Then come back here," I said, making a snap decision. "I'll let you in the house this time. I promise."

"No, it's not safe."

That was a switch. Was it possible that she didn't trust

us? "We aren't going to hurt you, Francie."

"Sorry. I've got to go," she said, and then she hung up on me.

"What was that all about?" Greg asked.

"I hate to ask, but can you kill that fire?"

My husband looked at the growing blaze, and then he frowned. "I guess I could. Is there a good reason to?"

"I think Francie might be in trouble. She could need our help."

Greg nodded, got up and grabbed a pitcher of ice water we kept in the fridge. After judiciously pouring it on the growing flames, I grabbed a towel and mopped up a little water that had escaped the fireplace. "I'm sorry we can't stay here and enjoy that."

"We'll do it soon," he said. "Now, I know that you and Moose are investigating this together, but I'm free right now. Can I go with you instead of your grandfather?"

I made an executive decision on the spot, and hoped that my grandfather would understand. "I'd like that a lot," I answered.

I didn't think there'd been any hesitation in my voice, but Greg must have sensed some. "Call Moose and get his blessing. It's the only way we're going to ever hear the end of it."

"You're right," I said and dialed my grandfather's number.

"Moose, Francie Humphries came by the house, but she took off before she'd tell us anything. Greg and I are going to go try to track her down. Are you okay with that?"

"Are you sure that you don't need me?" he asked.

"We can handle it," I assured him.

"Then give me a call after you've talked to her."

For some reason, that had just been too easy. "What's going on?"

"What do you mean?" he asked.

"I know you. There's no way in the world that you're okay with this, unless you know something that I don't."

"I don't think Francie did it," Moose admitted.

"What makes you so sure of that?"

Moose kept hesitating, and then finally, he said, "I happened to run into Pete Hampton on my way home from the diner." Pete was the one who'd been holding the birthday party for his daughter, the one Francie had been working on in the back of Iced alone.

"We'll talk about that particular odd coincidence in a second," I said. "What did Pete have to say?"

"He came by the bakery early to pick up the cupcakes, but it was clear that Francie wasn't done. Pete was afraid to go home, you know how his wife can be, so he stood outside and waited until they were finished."

"But she was in the back, working alone," I said.

"Yeah, but she must have left the door between the sales counter and the back open because Pete swears he saw her the entire time."

"So, she couldn't have killed Howard Lance," I said.

"No way. She's got a solid alibi, even if she doesn't realize it yet."

"And when exactly were you planning to tell me this, Moose? If I'd known that earlier, I wouldn't have been so cautious about letting Francie inside my house, and she wouldn't be out there right now feeling as though she were in serious danger before she could even tell me what was going on."

There was a long pause, and then my grandfather said, "To tell you the truth, I was saving it for morning. I messed up, didn't I, Victoria?"

He had indeed, but I wasn't about to rub it in. "Don't worry, Greg and I will find her."

"I'm going to go out looking, too. After all, it's kind of my fault that she might be in trouble right now. Should I come pick you two up, or should we split up and look separately?"

There was real merit in dividing our forces, but I hated to think that Moose might be out there somewhere by himself.

"Why don't you call Dad and have him join you?"

"I don't need your father to keep me company. I'm a grown man, remember?"

"Fine, have it your way, but if your pride keeps us from finding Francie in time, it's going to be squarely on your shoulders, Moose."

He took a deep breath, and then reluctantly said, "I'll go get him."

"Good, that's settled. And Moose, one more thing."

"What's that?"

"If you hear the slightest whisper about where Francie might be, you need to call me, and I mean immediately. Is that understood?"

"Yes, of course. I'm sorry, Victoria."

"Don't be sorry," I said, "Just don't do it again."

Greg was smiling when I got off the phone.

"What is it?" I asked him.

"Nothing at all," he said, stifling his grin. "Let's go."

Whatever it was, I decided to let it slide. "I'm ready. The only problem is that I don't know where to look."

Greg nodded as we walked out, and he locked the door behind us. I hated leaving our snug little nest for the chilly autumn air, but I didn't feel as though we had any real choice.

As Greg started the car, he said, "I've got a thought, but I'm afraid that it doesn't make any sense."

"Go on. Tell me anyway."

"Where do you think Francie feels safest in all of the world?"

"Do you think that she went home?"

Greg shook his head. "No, I'm talking about the bakery."

"Isn't that the first place someone would look for her if they really are after her?"

"Maybe, but would Francie realize that? What do we have to lose?"

"Not a thing in the world," I said. "Given that logic, let's check out her place first, since it's on the way."

"Sounds good to me."

"I hope you're right, Greg," I said, remembering how frightened Francie had sounded.

"You and me both."

Francie's place was dark when we got there, but Greg and I got out and checked anyway. After knocking on the front door repeatedly and ringing the bell, it was clear that if she were there, she wasn't coming out.

"Let's go to the bakery, then," Greg said.

The results there were different, much to my relief. As we parked down the block and walked toward her shop, I could see a hint of light coming from inside. As we neared the bakery, it was clear that Francie was in back. The door was cracked open just enough to see her sitting in one corner, slumped down in a chair. I banged on the door with my fist, but she didn't move.

Something was wrong.

"Greg, what should we do?"

"Don't panic," he said as he tried the front door, only to find it locked.

"I'm calling Sheriff Croft," I said as I grabbed my cell phone.

"Hold on a second," Greg said. "Let's go around back and try that door first."

I kept my phone in my hand as we made our way to the back of the shop. Guilt flooded through me for turning her away, and I knew that later I'd feel a flood of regret for my part in it, but for the moment, I just wanted to get to Francie to see what had happened to her.

"It's open," Greg said in surprise when he tried the door. We both rushed in to where Francie sat, and I called her name again as I reached out and touched her shoulder.

She jerked at the touch of my hand, and as her eyes opened wide, I saw the twin tracings of thin wire coming from the speakers in her ears. She had an iPod in, and had evidently cranked it up to its highest volume.

"What are you two doing here?" she asked as she pulled

the speaker bud out of her ears.

"What were you listening to?" I asked her.

"I had my Beethoven cranked all the way up," she said. "It soothes my nerves, but any good I got out of that is gone now. You nearly scared me blind just now."

"Sorry, but it was the only way to get your attention."

Francie looked around, and then asked, "How did you two even get in here?"

"The back door was unlocked," I said. "I thought you didn't feel safe."

"I have to latch it from inside, and sometimes it doesn't catch all the way," she said.

"What has you so spooked, Francie?" my husband asked her.

"I was reading a scary mystery novel, and all of a sudden, I had the feeling that someone was after me. I panicked, and that's when I came by your place."

"Why would someone be after you?"

She looked distressed as she admitted, "Come on, everyone in town thinks I might have killed that evil man."

"You shouldn't have to worry about that anymore," I said. "It turns out that you have an alibi after all."

"How is that possible?" she asked, clearly confused by my statement.

"Pete Hampton was out front watching you work. Let me guess, that latch doesn't work too well either, does it?"

She nodded. "Boy, am I ever glad I never got that fixed. So, is it true? I'm really in the clear?"

"That's how it sounds to us," Greg said.

"Does the sheriff know?" she asked.

"I don't know, but I'll find out right now." I called Moose, and he picked up on the second ring. Answering it, he said, "Your father is driving me crazy with questions. You talk to him."

Before I could protest, my dad was on the other end of the line. "Victoria, your grandfather is exasperating beyond belief."

"Join the club," I said. "Do me a favor and put him back on, Dad."

"She wants to talk to you, but only Heaven above knows why," I heard my dad say as he handed the phone back to his father.

"What is it?" Moose asked, the irritation plain to hear in his voice.

"We found Francie."

"Is she okay?" Moose asked quickly.

"She's fine, but she wants to know if Sheriff Croft knows about her alibi yet."

"I told Pete to call him," Moose said.

"Well, it might not be a bad idea to call the sheriff and make sure he got the message," I said.

"How am I going to explain to him how I knew about it?" Moose asked.

"That's your problem, isn't it? Call me as soon as you find out. We're staying with Francie until we know that it's all clear."

"I'll handle it," Moose said.

After I hung up, I asked, "Why don't we all stay right here together until we know for sure?"

"Thanks. I'd appreciate that," Francie said.

My husband spoke up a few minutes later as he pointed to a tray of iced cupcakes. "How much are those apiece?" he asked her.

"Greg, are you really that hungry?" I asked.

"Hey, I never had dessert tonight."

"Don't tell me that, I saw you sneaking a piece of apple pie as I was closing out the register report."

"It's not nice to spy on your husband," Greg said with a grin. "Besides, that was a new recipe I was trying out. Trust me, it was entirely work-related."

He looked so innocent in his protest that I had to laugh, and I knew that the battle was lost. "How much for two, Francie?" I asked with a grin.

"Actually, you both would be doing me a favor if you

tasted them for me. When I'm nervous, I bake, and lately, I've been baking like crazy trying out new flavors. I have four that you can choose from tonight."

"What are they?" Greg asked as he rubbed his hands together.

As she pointed to four separate rows, each in turn, she said, "This one's strawberry lime, this one's kiwi and mango, this is orange papaya, and the last one is just a new chocolate recipe I wanted to try out."

I knew without waiting for an answer which flavor my husband would choose. He loved chocolate as much as any woman I'd ever met. I reached for one of those and handed it to him.

"You know me pretty well, don't you?" he asked with a grin.

"I'd like to think so," I said as I grabbed one of the orange papaya flavors. With the first bite, I knew that I'd chosen poorly. The orange was there, though just barely. The papaya, however, was so overwhelming that I needed some water to wash its pungent presence out of my mouth.

Francie had been watching me closely, and she frowned as she saw my reaction. "The flavor's a little strong, isn't it?"

"And a bit unbalanced, as well," I said as I gulped down a glass of water.

"Was it really that bad, Victoria?" she asked.

"Oh, yes. What happened? Did you use an entire papaya in each cupcake?"

"No, but that's not off by much. Note to self, tone it down, and balance the flavors more."

I glanced over at Greg, who was carefully licking the wrapper of his cupcake now that the cake itself was gone.

"Was it that good?" I asked him.

He grinned like a little boy, even down to having a bit of chocolate icing on his chin, and then he said, "I'm not sure. I probably should try another before I give anyone my official opinion."

I laughed outright. "In your dreams." I turned to Francie then and said, "You've got a winner there."

"We'll take a dozen at the diner tomorrow," Greg said. We sometimes offered other treats at The Charming Moose, especially if it passed the taste test of being worthy, which evidently this one had.

"I wasn't trying to drum up more business," she protested.

"Then consider it a happy coincidence," Greg said as my cell phone rang.

Moose told me quickly that the sheriff was now aware of Francie's alibi, and had already confirmed it. As far as the police were concerned, she was in the clear.

"Does it feel better knowing that?" I asked her after I conveyed the news.

"More than I can tell you," she said.

"Francie, is there a possibility that you weren't being paranoid, and that someone really was out to get you?"

She laughed and waved it off. "No, I'm pretty sure that there's not a chance. Chalk it up to my overactive imagination."

"If you're sure," I said.

Greg took my hand. "You heard the lady, she's positive. Let's go home," he said.

I agreed, albeit a little reluctantly, but I knew that there was nothing else we could do tonight. As we drove back home, I told Greg, "Thanks for coming out with me tonight."

"Are you kidding? I got a cupcake out of the deal. I should be thanking you."

"Believe me, every questioning session I have with my suspects doesn't end with cupcakes."

"More's the pity," Greg said with a grin. "Do you still want to have that fire?"

"I thought we ruined it," I said.

"Give me ten minutes, and I'll have the wet wood out and a new blaze going. What do you say, Victoria?"

"I'm all for it."

I thought about the rest of our suspect list, and wondered if we were missing an opportunity to do more questioning since the diner was closed for the night, but in the end, I decided that my time with my husband was more important than what I might be able to find out with the little amount of time and energy I had left for that night.

Besides, I wasn't about to pass up the chance to snuggle in front of a fire with my husband. No matter how much time I spent with him at the diner, I cherished the nights we had alone at home, away from our customers, and even our family.

Chapter 13

"The Charming Moose," I said as I answered the telephone at the diner the next morning. I was waiting for Moose to get in so we could start digging again, but that didn't mean that I couldn't work the front until he showed up.

"Victoria, this is Cynthia Wilson. Do you have a second?"

I looked around the diner and saw that most of our customers were either waiting for their food, or happily eating their breakfasts. "Sure. What's up?"

"I hate to keep bringing this up, but I'm still worried about my business."

"Why, are customers not coming in anymore?"

"No, it's not that. I'm talking about those papers that Howard Lance served me," she answered.

"Have you been talking to Evelyn again?" Cynthia's mother was the very definition of a worrywart, and she'd definitely rubbed off on her daughter over the years.

"You know that we speak just about every night. She's still concerned, and honestly, so am I."

"Well, there's no reason to be. Howard's gone."

"Maybe so, but does anyone know if he has any heirs?"

"I have no idea," I admitted.

"Wouldn't it be prudent to find out?" she asked me. "What's to keep someone else from trying to steal our businesses now that Howard is gone?"

I took a deep breath, and tried to keep calm as I said, "That's just it. It was all just one big bluff, Cynthia. Howard Lance had no more right to our land than Captain Ahab."

"Who's that?" she asked, sounding worried yet again. "Is someone else going to try to evict us?"

"He's from Moby Dick," I said. "Surely you read that

book in school."

"I must have been sick that day," she said. Cynthia wasn't known as one of our town's great minds, but honestly, I had expected her to at least get that literary reference.

"What I'm trying to say is that the issue is dead." Much like Howard Lance, I could have added, but I didn't want to get Cynthia worked up again.

"I just wish I could believe that," she said. "Victoria, do you happen to know if he had any cash on him when he died?"

What an odd question that was. "I have no idea about that, either. Why do you ask?"

"I've just been wondering what he might do with the money if anybody actually paid him off to get rid of him."

"As far as I know, nobody did, though," I said.

"Okay. Woops, I've got to go. My nine o'clock appointment is here."

As I hung up, Bob Chastain walked in the door and hesitated at my station by the cash register. "Who was that?" he asked as lightly as he could. "I could hear the shrillness of her voice from all the way over here."

"Cynthia Wilson just called to chat," I said, not wanting to get into the status of one of my suspects with another of them.

"She always was as flighty as a hummingbird," Bob said.

"What brings you by for breakfast?" I asked him. Bob had lunch at our place every now and then, but as far as I knew, he never made it in for breakfast.

"I thought I'd shake things up a little. I heard the Moose Special was pretty good."

"It is, if you've got an appetite," I admitted.

"What all is on it?"

"All of my grandfather's favorite breakfast items," I said. "Two eggs, two pieces of toast, one pancake, one sausage patty or two strips of bacon, hash browns or grits, and a side of gravy."

"Wow, does anybody actually order that?" I knew that

Bob was proud of his weight loss, and I couldn't imagine him eating a third of what I'd just listed.

"You'd be surprised," I said as I pointed to a far table. Three gentlemen in their seventies were arguing about the price of turnips, in voices loud enough to rattle the windows. "They're all having the same meal."

"Somebody needs to tell them to quiet down," Bob said.

"They worked side by side in a factory for thirty years, and that was before anybody was concerned about hearing loss. They're good men who worked hard to support their families, and if they want to come in here and shout at each other once a week, I'm all for it."

"Sorry, I didn't know," Bob said. "They must take their cars somewhere else to get fixed. I don't work on Model Ts," he added with a grin.

"I happen to know for a fact that they fix their cars themselves."

"How could you know that?" Bob asked.

"They discussed it at length last week," I said with a smile. "They claimed that they were the last three shade-tree mechanics in all of Jasper Fork."

"They're probably not that far off," Bob said.

"Have you decided what you'd like to order?"

"How about a cup of coffee," he said, "to go."

"Are you sure that's going to hold you?"

"I'll be fine," he said.

I got him the coffee, rang him up, and then went into the kitchen after Bob was gone. "Did you see that?" I asked Greg.

"Sorry, I had one eye on the eggs and another on the bacon. I don't have much time to look around this time of day. What did I miss?"

"Bob Chastain came by for a cup of coffee, but I have a hunch he was looking for more than that."

"Did he get fresh with you, Victoria? I'll teach him a lesson about flirting with a married woman if I have to."

I couldn't tell if my husband was serious or not. He

didn't mind when I chatted with our customers, but if one got overly aggressive, he'd find an excuse to come out of the kitchen, likely as not sporting a butcher knife or some other sinister cooking tool.

"No, it was all perfectly harmless. Oh, Cynthia Wilson called me just before that, and she's still stressed out about Howard Lance's paperwork coming back to haunt every last one of us."

"You should know better than to listen to her," Greg said. "She's got a good heart, but it's not too difficult to upset her." He looked around, and then asked, "Hey, where's your partner in crime? I thought we'd see Moose around here by now, and your shift's over for now."

"I don't want to push him," I said. "You know how he likes to sleep in."

"I do not," Moose proclaimed loud enough to get the attention of even the retired factory workers. When they saw that it was just my grandfather, they went back to their discussion. I'd tuned them out before, and it wasn't hard to do it again. "I was working."

"On the case?" I asked softly. Was I going to have to discipline my own grandfather yet again? This was getting old really fast.

"In an indirect way," he admitted. Moose must have seen the storm clouds rolling across my face because he quickly added, "It was just a little preliminary telephone work. We need to take another truck ride, if you're ready."

"Where are we going this time?" I asked as I grabbed my jacket.

"We're headed back to Laurel Landing. I spoke with Happy, and he said that it might not be a bad idea for me to come by."

"You mean us, right?" I asked.

"I came here for you first, didn't I?" he asked. "What more can I do?"

I realized that I was being overly sensitive, but not because of any hurt feelings. I didn't want anything to happen to my grandfather, especially when I was so closely tied into what he was doing. I kissed his cheek, and then said, "I'm sorry about that."

He put one hand behind his right ear and asked, "Excuse me? I didn't quite get that. There was too much noise in the diner."

"Then you'll just have to do without hearing it again because I'm not about to repeat myself," I said with a smile.

Greg said, "I've got to get back to the kitchen. See you two later."

"You can count on it," I said as I grabbed my jacket. "Well, are we leaving, or are we just going to stand around the rest of the morning?"

Moose started to protest when he saw my grin. "You'll be the death of me yet, granddaughter."

"I sincerely hope not," I said, and we started for the door.

We never made it out, though.

Someone was blocking our way, and I wasn't all that excited to see him.

"We were just leaving," I said as I tried to sidestep our sheriff.

"Where are you both off to now?" he asked, "or do I really want to know?"

"How about a little 'don't ask-don't tell' at the moment?" I asked.

The sheriff just shook his head. "Let's forget about that. I need to talk to you, Moose."

My grandfather looked surprised. "What's going on, Sheriff? I've been completely honest with you."

"I don't doubt it. This isn't a bad visit. I just wanted to come by and personally thank you for sending Pete Hampton my way last night. That was a fine thing you did there."

Moose explained, "I shouldn't get all of the credit. Victoria here is the one who put it all in motion."

For some reason, that seemed to surprise the sheriff. He looked at me and tipped his hat slightly. "Then I'll thank you as well. That had to help Francie's peace of mind."

"I wish it could help everyone else's," I said. The second the last word left my lips I knew that it had been a mistake, but it was too late to retract now. Maybe the sheriff would just let it go.

Not likely, though. "Who else would we be talking about?"

I thought about trying to stonewall him, but I knew that all that would do was raise Moose's blood pressure, and still not get us anywhere. "Cynthia Wilson called here earlier. She's still concerned that someone else is going to come along and try to take her hair salon. Evidently Evelyn is getting her riled up, and you know how that can be."

The sheriff nodded. "I'll stop by later and have a word with her."

"She asked me something intriguing," I added. "Maybe you can answer it for me, since I don't have a clue."

"What is it?"

"Did you find any cash around Howard Lance, either on him, or at his place?" It was a touchy subject bringing up Howard's apartment, but I really wanted to know.

"As a matter of fact," the sheriff said, "We found nearly ten grand in his place stashed under his mattress."

I let the fact pass that he hadn't told us about it. "Any idea where he got the money?"

"A few," Sheriff Croft said cagily. "How about you?"

"At least one person must have paid him off," I said.

Moose's eyebrows shot up, but he didn't comment. After a few seconds, the sheriff nodded. "Yeah, that's what I think, too. Any ideas who might have done it?"

"Sheriff, I'm not even sure who could have raised that kind of cash on such short notice. I was kind of hoping that you'd know."

"Well, it's no big secret that it's impossible to trace cash," the sheriff said, "but we're looking into it. Anything else?"

"Who gets the money now?" I asked him.

"What do you mean?"

"I'm just wondering if anyone else had a motive to kill Howard Lance. Did he leave some kind of fortune behind, and was it motive enough to kill him?"

"No fortune, at least as far as we've been able to find. As to heirs, none have turned up yet. I have a hunch that what we found was all he had, but I've been wrong before." He stretched his neck a little, and then asked, "Anybody else call you?"

"No, but Bob Chastain came to the diner for breakfast, and to my knowledge, he's never done that before."

"Did he grill you about the case?" the sheriff asked.

"No, he kind of made it a point not to ask."

The sheriff shook his head. "If you're going to start bringing me negative information, this could take awhile."

"No, that's it," I said, trying my best to smile.

Moose asked, "Have you heard from Hank and Margie yet?"

Sheriff Croft shook his head. "No, but we'll track them down sooner or later. I can't figure out why they'd run like that. It just makes them look guilty of something."

"But not necessarily of murder," I said.

"No, I'm reserving judgment until I have more information," he said.

"If you're done with us, Moose and I have an errand to run," I said.

"Is there any point in me following you to see what the two of you are up to today?" the sheriff asked.

"You could always try," Moose said with a broad grin, "but you'll never catch us. There's more to my truck than meets the eye."

"I know all about how you had the engine beefed up," the sheriff said. "Just don't break any speed limits, you hear me? I'd hate to have to write you up after coming by here especially so I could thank you."

"I'd hate that, too," Moose said. "I'm glad we have an understanding."

"We have nothing of the sort," the sheriff said with a smile.

Moose didn't answer; he just waved and shoved me out the door.

"Do you think he's going to actually follow us to Laurel Landing?" I asked once we were in Moose's truck driving away.

"If he does, I'm going to lead him on the goosiest wild goose chase he's ever seen."

When we got to the BBQ Pit, Happy was waiting by the door for us. "I'm glad you're here," he said as he shook our hands in turn.

"What's so urgent that we had to drive all this way?" Moose asked.

"I never said it was urgent," Happy said. "You always did over-exaggerate everything, you old goat."

"So, are you telling me that we dropped everything and drove all this way for nothing?"

"It's not nothing," Happy said. He turned to his servers and said, "Stacy, Josephine, I need you both over here, right now."

The two women glared at each other, and then their boss, but they came nonetheless. "What is it, Happy? I have customers."

"So do I," Stacy snapped. "You're no more important around here than I am."

"I never said that I was," Josephine cracked right back.

"Both of you, pipe down!" Happy said.

To my amazement, both of them dropped into instant silence. Honestly, I think that Happy was a little bit amazed himself, but he must have known that it wasn't going to last long. "Tell us what you two were doing when Howard was murdered."

"How are we supposed to know that?" Josephine asked.

"If you had ever loved the man, you wouldn't have to ask," Stacy said. She turned to Hap and said, "I was here, working."

"Then I was here, too," Josephine replied. "We've both been working the same shift for the past two weeks." Then she turned back to Stacy and added, "For your information, I know when he was murdered, at least down to the half hour. What I was trying to say was that I didn't know the exact time, and from what I've heard, neither do the police. The only way you'd know is if you were the one who did it."

"Take that back," Stacy snapped, her temper coming back in full force.

Happy stepped between them to stop any real fight before it had a chance to get started. "I told you both I had to keep you together while I'm looking for another waitress. Believe me, I'm looking, but for now, you need to find a way to get along."

"Are you giving them both alibis?" Moose asked.

"Sure, and I would have told you straight out the last time you were here, but you seemed more interested in my smoker than you did in Howard's murder."

I made it a point not to make eye contact with my grandfather, or alter my expression in any way.

"How can you be so sure?" Moose said.

"It's a long drive to Jasper Fork and back. Trust me, if one of them was gone for more than two minutes that day, I'd have noticed. But I happen to have a more definitive reason than you've heard so far. It involves a plate of onion rings, and two very angry customers."

That seemed to start the squabble again. "Those were for my order!" Stacy said loudly.

"In your dreams, cupcake," Josephine replied. "I'd been waiting for them seven minutes, and you just showed up at the window, grabbed them, and took off like you owned the place."

"That's because I ordered them two minutes before you even got to the window, Jo." She said the last bit with a gleam in her eye, and I was getting ready to step out of their line of fire.

"Don't call me Jo!"

Happy glared at them in turn, and then said in a soft voice, "So help me, if I hear one more word out of either one of you, I'll cook and wait tables myself until I can find replacements for the both of you."

"You can't handle this place without help," Josephine said, breaking Happy's declaration of silence.

"It won't be for long, and by then it won't be any concern of either one of you. Now, are we all going to have a truce around here, or are things about to get very ugly? I don't even know why you're still fighting. You should be looking to find strength in each other with Howard gone. We all know that he wasn't the world's greatest prize, but you both cared for him, even if you won't admit it to the world. The choice is pretty easy; make up, or hit the road. I mean it."

I wasn't sure which server would be the first to act, but I was still surprised when Josephine put out her hand to the other. "Truce."

Without any hesitation, Stacy took it, nodded, and echoed the sentiment. After a moment, she said, "I loved him, but he could be a real pain in the pants, couldn't he?" She added a slight grin to take the sting out of her words.

"More than anyone else could probably ever realize but the two of us," Josephine nodded, smiling a little herself.

"Let me buy you a sweet tea," Stacy said, "and we'll drink to the old rascal's memory."

"Okay, but I should be the one buying," Josephine said. "After all, I was his ex-wife."

Happy could sense the threat of a return to hostility, so he quickly said, "How about if I buy? We'll all toast the old so and so together."

Both women turned on him at once, and Josephine said, "There's no need to speak ill of the dead, Happy."

"Yeah," Stacy said. "He might have been a slimy creature sometimes, but he was our slimy creature."

They walked to the counter, got two glasses, filled them with tea, and then drank to their dead common interest together.

Moose said softly, "That was pretty well done, even if it was in your own unique backhanded kind of way."

"Thanks. I thought it worked out pretty well myself. Maybe now that they've gotten it all out in the open, they'll be able to get along."

"I hope so," I said, "but I wouldn't count on it. Thanks for calling us, Happy."

"I should be thanking you," he said.

Moose and I decided to leave while things were still on a good note there. Back in his truck, he asked, "Should we head back home now?"

"Sure, but let's make a stop on the way."

"Where are we going?" he asked.

"I want to talk to Monica Ingram again," I said.

Moose shook his head. "Be my guest, but you wouldn't mind if I waited for you in the truck, would you?"

I had to laugh. "What's the matter? You're not afraid of a woman, are you?"

"It's not the 'woman' part that makes me nervous," he said. "The part that I'm wary of is the part that's an attorney. Lawyers and I never did seem to get along."

"Go on, wait in the truck, then," I said with a laugh as he pulled up in front of Monica's building. "But don't wander off. I don't even know if she's free."

"Then why talk to her?" Moose asked.

"There's a question Sheriff Croft couldn't answer that I want to know."

"About Lance's heirs?" Moose asked. "Even if she knows, what makes you think that she'll tell you any more than she did before?"

"Just call it a hunch. What's the worst that can happen?"

Moose just shook his head. "I stopped asking myself that question a long time ago when I kept getting answers that I didn't like."

Pulled pork sandwiches by Victoria's mother, Melinda

This recipe couldn't be easier, and though it doesn't smoke the meat like Moose would like, it's still mouthwateringly good on sandwiches, or as a main course! We use a slow cooker for this one, and it's a wonderful meal to make, especially if you're going to be near the kitchen all day. The delightful aroma alone is enough to knock you off your feet!

Ingredients

3-4 lbs. Boston Butt roast (or comparable cut of meat)
Salt and pepper for seasoning
1 medium onion, yellow or white, diced
18 oz. (or comparable) bottle barbeque sauce

Directions

You can spray the cooker's pot itself, or use a slow cooker cooking bag for virtually no mess. Rub the meat with a teaspoon each of salt and pepper, and then put it in the base of the slow cooker, the fat side up. Next, dice the onion, add it to the pot, and then add the barbeque sauce, covering the meat with it. There will be some left in the bottom of the bottle, so put that into the refrigerator for later.

Cover the slow cooker, set the temperature to LOW for 8 hours and cook, or until the meat is tender to the touch of a fork. On a separate plate, remove the meat (pieces at this point will fall apart at the touch), discard the fat and bone, and then pull the remaining meat between two forks until you have a nice consistency. Don't overwork it at this stage, or you'll get something that more resembles chopped pork, something you want to avoid.

Add some of the sauce back to this finished mix of pulled pork, in equal parts from the bottle and what is in the Crockpot.

Enjoy!

Chapter 14

"I didn't expect to see you again so soon," Monica Ingram said as I walked into her office. She was unboxing some kind of playpen and wrestling with it in an attempt to set it up in one corner.

"I didn't realize you had children. Monica, do you even have a secretary?" I asked her with a smile.

"She's out on maternity leave," Monica admitted. "Thus the playpen. It's been kind of hectic around here, but she's coming back to work tomorrow. That's why I got her this. Do you think she'll like it?"

"If you're letting her bring her newborn to work, I think she'll love it."

Monica nodded. "It was the only way I could get her to come back after having the baby. It might be a little disruptive, but it can't be worse than how it's been with her gone, can it?"

"I reserve judgment, based on a complete and utter lack of experience or knowledge in the matter," I said.

"You sound like you've got a little attorney blood in your veins yourself," Monica answered with a grin.

"That's because I've probably spent too much time hanging out with my best friend," I admitted. "Rebecca has a tendency sometimes to use twenty words when four will do."

"She sounds like my kind of gal," Monica said. She stared at the pen for another second, and then stood. "I give up. I'm hoping that Lisa knows how to put this thing together because I for one am lost."

"You could always just read the directions," I said as I pointed to a sheet of paper on the floor.

"I'm too much my father's daughter to even consider it," she answered. "I'm glad you came by. I was just going to call you."

"What's going on?"

She reached toward the top of the desk and pulled some papers from it. "I just filed this earlier, so it's now a matter of public record."

"What is it?" I asked, but then got my answer as I scanned it quickly. "This is Howard Lance's will."

"It is, though I don't know why he bothered. Then again, he paid me good money to write it, and I wasn't about to turn him down."

"So, you didn't get stiffed? That's good."

"It's just good business. Cash and carry, that's always been my policy."

I looked at the pages of legalese, and then I handed it all back to her. "Can you just give me the highlights? Legal jargon gives me the hives."

"I'm glad I don't have that particular affliction," she said. "Basically, what it boils down to is that anything that's left over from his holdings after paying off his bills goes to two women here in town."

"Let me guess, Josephine and Stacy from the BBQ Pit."

She smiled at me. "So, you took my advice after all."

"It was excellent, but it didn't do me any good. They were both working when Howard was murdered, and apparently there are a dozen witnesses to prove it."

"That's good to know," she said, "but even if they were both still suspects in your mind, money wasn't a motivating factor. Howard was a good thirty thousand dollars in debt when he died."

"Then the ten thousand dollars the police found of his wouldn't even touch it."

Monica nodded. "I knew about that, but I wasn't certain that you did. You're well connected around here, aren't you?"

"It's as much my grandfather as it is me," I said.

"Where is the charming old gentleman?" Monica asked, and I couldn't say for sure if she was joking or not.

"He's waiting for me in the truck. I think you might

intimidate him a little."

That got a full-on laugh. "That's too much. Let me walk you out so I can say hello to him myself."

"I'd enjoy that," I said as I followed her outside. Moose was doing a crossword puzzle from the newspaper, something not at all odd to find. He kept a stack of them in his truck to occupy himself in his downtime.

He was clearly startled as we approached. "I'm hurt you didn't come in," Monica told him with a smile.

"I had something to take care of," Moose said.

"I'll bet. Thirty-six down is 'Flowing,' by the way."

Moose looked at the puzzle, and then said, "No, it's not. It's 'Rascal.'"

"My mistake," she answered. "I guess it takes one to know one." She patted the truck's hood as I got in, and waved at us both as we drove away.

"Why did you let her come out?" Moose asked.

"What was I going to do, tackle her to keep her from seeing you? It's not like you to act this way toward any woman you've ever met," I said.

"I'll admit it. She throws me a little off," Moose said. "Did you find out anything from her?"

"Apparently Howard Lance left a will, but there was no money to cover his bequests. You're not going to believe who his main two beneficiaries were."

"Unless it's our two waitress friends, I give up," Moose said.

"I guessed that, too, but you're right," I said, a little miffed that my grandfather had come to the same conclusion that I had.

"Where to now, Victoria?" my grandfather asked.

"We have a few options," I said after a moment's thought. "We can try to corner Cynthia or Bob again, or we can keep looking for Hank and Margie. Those are the only suspects we have left, as far as I'm concerned."

"I say we go to Cynthia's," Moose said. "She sounded kind of jumpy this morning from what you told me about her telephone call."

"That sounds good to me. I wouldn't know where to even start looking for Hank and Margie, anyway. I just can't see them together, can you?"

"Love doesn't always make sense to anyone who's in it," Moose said, "but it's never something you can afford to just ignore."

"Who knew my grandfather could be such a romantic?" I asked as we headed back to Jasper Fork.

"You could have always just asked my wife," Moose said with a smile. "If anyone knows me, it's your grandmother."

"How do you do it after all these years?" I asked.

"I've got a suspicion you know. I've watched you and Greg. You two are going to stick for life, just like Martha and I have."

"How about my mom and dad?" I asked.

"They've got it, too. I haven't entirely approved of everything your father has done on this earth, but marrying your mother was the smartest thing he ever managed. We may not have fame or fortune, but our family knows how to find love, and when it comes down to it, what is there that could be more valuable?"

I shook my head as I smiled. "They don't call you The Charming Moose for nothing, do they?"

"Actually, that's what the diner is called," he said with the hint of a smile.

"Do you mean the one that's named after you?" I asked him.

"Purely coincidence," he said, and then couldn't hold his laughter in any longer.

When we got to the salon, the shades were still pulled and it was dark inside. I was afraid that we had another runner when I remembered what day it was. "She's not here."

"I can see that for myself," Moose said.

"No, I mean ever. This is her afternoon off, and she takes it every week. We could always go by her house to see if she's there."

"No, doing that will just spook her," Moose said. "We've already questioned her here. If we go by her place, she's going to have a heart attack."

"Then let's try Bob," I suggested.

"I'm game," Moose said, and drove there quickly. At least they were open for business.

Bob looked up from his desk as we walked into his office. He'd been doodling on his calendar, drawing birds of all things. Was he that bored, or was something on his mind? "Has that old death-trap of yours finally given up the ghost?" he asked my grandfather.

"Don't count on it. She's as strong as the day is long," Moose said proudly.

"One of these days you're going to need me," Bob answered with a grin.

"But not today," Moose shot back quickly. "I'm sorry I missed you at the restaurant this morning."

He glanced straight at me. "Victoria, I didn't realize that my visit had been all that significant enough to tell your grandfather about," he said good-naturedly.

"What can I say? It was a slow news morning."

"It must have been. Don't read anything into it, though. I thought a big breakfast might be good for a change of pace, but I couldn't bring myself to do it. This diet has me paranoid about every single bite I put into my mouth." He paused for a moment, but before Moose or I could ask him anything else about the murder, Nancy Barton came storming into his office. "The smell is getting worse."

I glanced at her, at Moose, and then sniffed the air.

She caught me doing it. "Not in here, Victoria, in my car." Nancy turned back to Bob and said, "You told me that you fixed it."

"Nancy, I'll be happy to have one of the guys look at it for you again."

"No," she said firmly. "You are coming with me, and I mean right now." She glanced at us and said, "I'm sorry to interrupt, but my sister and I are driving to Atlanta this evening, and I can't abide that noxious odor."

"Sorry," Bob said as he got up from his desk, "but duty calls."

Before either one of us could say another word, Bob and Nancy were gone.

"We're not having much luck today, are we?" I asked my grandfather.

"Not one single bit," he said.

"What's left?" I asked.

"There's nothing we can do but go back to the diner."

I agreed, but not grudgingly at all. It was where I belonged, not out chasing down leads that never paid off. I still wanted to find the murderer who had crept into our diner and struck, but there was no use beating our heads against the wall until something else turned up. If and when it did, I'd be happy to drop everything and start hunting for clues again, but in the meantime, I was going to get back to work.

"What are you still doing here?" I asked Ellen as Moose and I walked into the diner. "You should have been home an hour and a half ago."

"Your grandmother had an errand to run, and I promised Greg that I'd hang around," she said, though I knew that she was already late meeting her kids.

"What about the guys?"

"I had Myra Greene get them from the bus stop. She loves them almost as much as I do, and they never get tired of going over to her place, especially since she makes them Snickerdoodle cookies."

"Well, I really appreciate it, but you can take off now."

"Thanks," she said as she grabbed her coat and took off.

"You're back," Greg said with a smile when I walked into the kitchen to place an order. Jenny would be there soon and I could take over the register alone, but for now, I was working the floor and the front.

He hugged me, but then quickly let go.

"Why so brief?" I asked, but Greg was already headed out into the dining room, the meat cleaver he'd been holding still grasped firmly in his hand.

"Where do you think you're going?" he asked a young man in jeans and a worn old T-shirt as he was hurriedly heading for the exit.

"I'm finished," the guy said.

"I hope you enjoyed it, but you still need to pay for your meal."

"I gave my money to the other lady," he said, casting his glance downward.

Greg approached him, holding the cleaver out from his body, as though it were a pistol in a holster that he was preparing to draw.

"There's a simple way to prove that. If your ticket is on the pin, I'll buy your next meal here on the house, whatever you want."

"And if it's not?" the kid asked warily.

"Then I'll collect in whatever way that I can."

I expected him to take his chances and run, but instead, the kid broke down. "Mister, I'd pay if I could, but I'm flat broke. I'm sorry. I don't want to steal, but I don't have much choice."

"What's your name?" my husband asked him.

"Mike," he admitted.

"Let me ask you something, Mike. Are you physically able to work?" Greg asked, his voice still calm.

"Yes, sir," the young man reluctantly. "But nobody will give me a chance."

"Follow me," Greg said.

Mike hesitated, but then he did as my husband ordered. Greg came back out a few minutes later.

"What happened?"

"I put him to work moving those crates in back that have been bugging me for weeks. I was determined to do it myself tonight after work, but why not let Mike do it and give him a chance to pay for his meal?"

"What's to keep him from just running away?" I asked. "That back alley isn't exactly locked up."

"Well, young Michael and I had a little talk, and I believe that he'll do as he promised."

"And if he doesn't?" I asked.

"Then we'll never be bothered with him again. It's as elegant a solution as I could ask for."

"You're a good man, Greg," I said as I kissed my husband's cheek.

"Don't forget, I know what it's like to be hungry," he said, and then turned back to his grill. My husband had lived with his mother after her divorce from his father, and there had been times she and Greg had gone without food, or even a roof over their heads. It was something that stayed with Greg every day, and he was eternally grateful for every meal, every shower, and every night he slept in a nice, soft bed.

It was nearing the end of the day with no more excitement of any kind when I asked Greg, "Have you checked up on Mike yet?"

"No, I told him to come back in when he was finished," Greg told me.

"Well, he's running out of time," I said as I glanced at the clock. "We're shutting the place down in twelve minutes."

"Don't worry about it. We'll deal with it then," he said.

Four minutes to closing, Mike came back in, dirty and tired, but smiling. "I got them all moved," he told Greg. "Come out and see for yourself."

"Good man," Greg told him. "I trust you," my husband added as he handed him a large brown paper bag. "There's a meatloaf sandwich in there, some chips, and a drink."

"I can't take it," Mike said reluctantly. "You were right. I don't want to be that guy anymore. If I can't pay for it, I don't want it."

Greg nodded. "Moving those crates paid for two meals, and a cash bonus to boot," he said as he reached into his wallet and pulled out a twenty dollar bill. "Nicely done."

"Do you need anything done around here tomorrow?" he asked Greg.

"No, not at the diner, but go see this man," he said as he handed the young man a piece of paper. "He might be able to help you out. He's a good man, Mike. You can trust him."

"Thanks," he said, and then quickly left the restaurant.

"Did you give him Father Randy's number?" I asked.

Greg nodded. "I called him earlier, and he's got room tonight at the shelter."

"Aren't you the least bit curious if Mike did the job the way you wanted him to?"

"We'll see soon enough," Greg said as he started cleaning up the back.

"You don't want to know if he failed you, do you?" I asked.

My husband didn't answer, and I found myself hoping that this wayward young man had held up his end of the deal. Greg believed in people, and always expected the best of them. Usually they tried to live up to his expectations, but sometimes they let him down, taking advantage of his good nature, and killing a bit of his spirit along the way.

I held my breath as we shut off the lights and closed the diner. As we walked out through the back door, I could see that the pallets had been moved perfectly in the glow of the light we had back there.

I half expected Greg to say something about it, but he just smiled a little and nodded with pleasure.

If Mike ever came back to the diner again, the next meal was going to be on me.

I figured my husband's smile had been worth that, and a whole lot more.

Chapter 15

In my dream, a telephone was ringing, and without giving it another thought, I picked it up and said, "Hello."

"Victoria, you need to come to the diner right now," the man said in a commanding voice on the other end of the line, and I knew that it wasn't a dream after all. I didn't recognize whoever was talking, but then again, in my defense, I wasn't used to getting calls at three in the morning.

"Who is this?" I asked as I rubbed my eyes with my free hand.

"I knew I should have called Moose first," he said, and at that moment I realized that it was Sheriff Croft.

"That's fine. I'm here. I'm awake," I said as I sat up. Greg, being the bear that he was, hadn't even stirred when my phone had rung. "What's wrong? Did something happen?"

"You could say that. Somebody just tried to burn the diner down tonight."

I beat Moose to the diner by four minutes, even though he was still in his pajamas, while I'd taken the time to throw on a pair of jeans and an old sweatshirt. Sheriff Croft had already briefed the two of us, so Greg met my grandfather at his truck before the man could start yelling at everyone in sight. "Take it easy, Moose. The fire's out. Somebody threw a lit skull through the front window and tried to set the place on fire."

"A skull? You're kidding me. Was it real?"

"No, of course not. It was just a replica. This one was made of resin. It's some kind of Halloween decoration, from the look of it."

"Then what started the fire?" Moose asked as he headed for the front of the diner. We all had no choice but to follow him.

The sheriff stepped in and blocked him. "It looks as though they coated the thing in lighter fluid before they threw it through the window. Nothing inside got scorched all that much. My guess is that it was pretty much out by the time it went through the window."

Moose walked around the sheriff and checked out the glass. After that, he walked in through the front door as though nothing had happened. The sheriff had told me that he'd gotten a few pictures before I got there, bagged the skull in an evidence bag, and then he'd encouraged me to clean the mess up.

I knew that Moose would want to see it for himself, though, so I hadn't touched a thing.

"Somebody better clean that up," he said after he surveyed the mild amount of damage.

Greg stepped past me. "I'm on it."

"Who would do something like this?" I asked.

"Most likely it's just a prank, but they went a little too far this time," the sheriff said. "Halloween is just around the corner, and if this is any indication, I'm going to be busy putting out fires all over town." He must have realized how that sounded, given what had just happened at the diner. "Not real fires, I mean." As an afterthought, Sheriff Croft added, "At least I hope not."

"You don't think this was deliberate, do you?" Moose asked.

"Well, I doubt it was an accident," the sheriff said.

"That's not what he meant, and you know it," I said. "I think someone is trying to scare us off of our investigation."

"How do you see it that way?" the sheriff asked. "Is there anything, and I mean anything, that would lead you to believe that's true?"

"Are you telling me that a flaming skull thrown through our front window isn't enough for you?" I asked him.

"Where's the note, Victoria, the threatening message that ties in with anyone involved in the case? If you want my opinion, this is most likely just a random act of vandalism."

"Hang on," Moose said. "Victoria's got a point. You don't see something like this every day of the week."

"No, but it's not very specific if it really is a warning, is it? How are you supposed to know who it is exactly you're supposed to be leaving alone?"

"What if it's meant for our entire investigation?" I asked.

"No offense, but I think you're both flattering yourselves. What we have here is most likely some angry teenager who's got a grudge against you. Have you run across anybody like that lately?"

Greg spoke up for the first time. "Mike didn't do this."

"How can you be so sure?" I asked him.

Moose demanded, "Who's this Mike character, and why would he want to firebomb our diner?"

I brought them all up to date, but I ended with, "He and Greg worked things out. There's no way that young man would do this."

"Maybe he was just playing you, or he could have had second thoughts about the worthiness of the punishment you gave him."

"I didn't punish him," Greg said firmly, "I tried to give him a job so he could feel good about something in his life for once."

The sheriff shrugged. "Maybe he didn't appreciate the life lesson. Did you happen to get this kid's last name?"

"I don't have a clue what it is," Greg said.

While that was true, I had a good idea where the young man was spending the night, but if Greg didn't want to volunteer the information, I wasn't about to do it, either. Besides, I agreed with my husband. There was no way, unless the young man was schizophrenic, that he could ever do something like this.

"How about you?" the sheriff asked me.

"I didn't catch his last name, either," I admitted.

"Okay. Still, just to be on the safe side, I'd keep an eye out for him if I were you."

Moose asked, "Do you think whoever did this might actually come back here again tonight?"

"It's highly doubtful," the sheriff said. "Just be on your guard." He looked at the broken window, and then asked, "Do you have any plywood or anything you could cover this with until you can get the glass replaced?"

"We've still got some plywood in the backroom from when Hurricane Hugo came through here," Greg said. "I'll go grab a sheet."

"I'll help," Moose said.

After they disappeared into the backroom, I asked the sheriff, "Do you honestly believe that this was just random?"

"More than likely," he said. "But who have you pushed around lately about Howard Lance's murder, whether you've cleared them of the crime in your mind or not?"

"Sheriff, you know our list as well as we do. There's Bob Chastain, Cynthia Wilson, the two waitresses from Laurel Landing, Hank and Margie, and Francie Humphries."

He frowned as he heard my recitation. "Surely you can narrow that down some by now. Let me put it this way. Who's still on your list of suspects? Don't bother telling me who you've already eliminated."

"All we have left are Bob, Cynthia, Hank, and Margie. How about you?" I asked with a slight grin. Maybe the sheriff felt like sharing. It was at least worth a shot.

"They're all on mine as well," he admitted.

"Who else, though?"

"Nobody you need to worry about," he said.

"That might be true, but I still believe that this vandalism is tied into our investigation of Howard Lance's murder."

"You're welcome to think whatever you'd like to," the sheriff said, "but as far as I'm concerned, and until I learn differently, this one's going down in the books as a random act of violence."

"Do you honestly believe that? If it were a brick that wasn't on fire being thrown through our window, I might agree with you, but a flaming skull? Come on."

"I've said my piece," he said. "Now, if you don't need me anymore here, I have a stray deputy I need to track down. That's how I happened to see your window in the first place. I believe that one of my people is using the nightshift to catch up on some sleep, and if I find out that it's true, I'm firing them on the spot, no questions asked."

"That's kind of harsh, isn't it?"

"Victoria, I'm responsible for this town, and one chance is all that anybody ever gets to let me down. Good night."

"Night," I echoed. "Thanks for calling me."

"You're welcome."

Once he was gone, my husband and grandfather reappeared with plywood and an electric screwdriver/drill. "Don't worry about the window, Victoria. We'll have this plywood up in no time," Greg said.

"Good. Then maybe we can go back home and get some sleep before we have to open the place up later."

"Do you honestly think that you can sleep after this?" my husband asked me.

"You know me better than that. I'm the second best sleeper I know."

He grinned sheepishly at me. "I'm willing to bet that I come in first place."

"Actually, it's a tie between you and Moose."

My grandfather shook his head as his name came up in the conversation. "Leave me out of this. Lift your end a little higher, Greg."

As my husband complied, Moose drove a screw home, and then another, and another. By the time they were finished, the blocked opening offered more protection than mere glass ever had.

It took a while for me to get back to sleep once Greg and I were home and in bed again, but I finally managed to nod off. I wasn't all that sure that it had been worth it, though. Flaming skulls of all sizes kept chasing me through my dreams, with glass swans swooping up and down above them, and I wondered if they were all trying to tell me something.

If they had, I was afraid to admit that it was all lost on me.

Before I knew it, I was in the middle of my first shift at the diner, and my mother was in the kitchen. Greg was sleeping in, but then again, he normally didn't get started until eleven. The Charming Moose was crowded with folks grabbing a bite before they headed off to work. By the time I was ready to take my first break at eight, most of them had cleared out, at least those going to regular jobs. Moose was usually nowhere to be found at the diner at that time of morning, but today was special. It was the monthly meeting of the Liar's Table, and my grandfather never missed a chance to participate. The collection of four men and one woman were at their reserved table, and as I passed by, I topped off their coffee mugs.

As I did, I heard my dentist, Dr. Frye, saying, "That trout was so big he pulled my boat around the lake three times before he wore himself out. It took four men to get him into the boat, but he was so heavy, we capsized. Luckily I'd brought along the heavy duty cooler, you know, the one that floats? We all climbed aboard and made our way to shore."

"What did you use for paddles?" Moose asked, as straight-faced as he could be.

"We didn't need them. I used my rod to catch a heron that happened to be flying by, and he towed us in himself."

Moose nodded, satisfied with the explanation. Everyone else had already gone, each in turn trying to top the other, and now my grandfather was up. I loved his stories, and there was no one in North Carolina who could fib as well as he could. He'd taught me at his knee the difference between a lie and a fib, and I still lived by it myself. A fib was a harmless stretching of the truth, sometimes beyond recognition, but there was no malice in it. It was something that, on the proper occasion, could even be admired. A lie, on the other hand, was an untruth told to hurt someone else, and we didn't stand for that around the diner.

"Well, I was going to tell you about when my son and I were up at the lodge fishing ourselves, but I'm afraid that Doc stole most of that thunder."

The winner had his breakfast paid for by the rest of the crew gathered, and Doc Frye looked as though he was about to collect when Moose added, "Thunder reminds of lightning, though. Did I ever tell you all about the time I was electrocuted seven times between the lake and my cabin's front door? The first six hits kind of stung a bit, but the last one hit me so hard that my ears shot out like a pair of rabbit-ear antennas. Whenever I closed my eyes, I could pick up stations as far away as Charlotte on a clear day."

"Did it just wear off on its own, or did you do something special to kill it?" Thelma Johnson asked, the only woman allowed at the table, at least so far.

"Now I ask you," Moose asked, "why would I ever want to get rid of it? It's a great way to keep up with the news, and whenever there's bad weather coming, I know exactly how to act."

"Do you run and hide inside so you don't get hit again?" Doc Frye asked.

"Just the opposite, in fact. I'm hoping the next time I get a direct hit, I'll be able to pick up ESPN."

They each threw a few dollars into the pot. Moose's story was good, but today, Doc Frye took the prize.

"Sorry you lost," I told Moose after he left the table.

He lowered his voice and explained, "I try to lose on purpose every now and then just to keep them all coming back. After all, it wouldn't be fair to win it every week."

"So, do you actually have a topper for Doc Frye's story?" I asked.

"As a matter of fact, I do. I was hiking on the Appalachian Trail once and…"

I never did get to hear the end of that particular lie.

Moose was interrupted by a pair of folks we'd been

looking for since just after the murder. All of our efforts had been in vain, but somehow, Hank and Margie had managed to walk into the diner all on their own.

"Where have you two been?" I asked as I approached them. "We've been looking everywhere for you."

"Why in the world would you want to do that?" Hank asked, a happy grin on his face.

"You should know better," Moose said.

"Know better than what?" he asked, clearly confused by the turn the conversation had just taken.

"Hank, you two can't be in the middle of a murder investigation and just take off like that," Moose said. "Surely you both must realize how guilty it makes you look."

Hank and Margie were clearly stunned by Moose's comment. "Murder? Who was murdered?"

"You haven't heard about what happened?" I asked, incredulous to hear it.

"Not even a whisper." He turned to Margie and asked, "Did you know anything about a murder?"

"I'm as surprised as you are, Hank," she said as she looked at me. "Who exactly was murdered, Victoria?"

"Someone killed Howard Lance in our freezer," I said.

Hank shook his head, as though he didn't believe it. "When exactly did this happen?"

When I told him, he let out a sigh of relief. "Why are you so happy?" I asked him.

"Margie and I were on a plane to Vegas, and we can prove it."

"Why did you two go to Vegas?" Moose asked him.

Margie answered for him, holding up her ring finger. "We eloped!" She studied me for a second, and then asked me, "Victoria, you're not surprised at all, are you?" She was clearly disappointed with my reaction. "You couldn't have known, though. We just decided ourselves."

"No, of course not. Congratulations," I said. In a way, I was a little taken aback. After all, dating and getting married were two different things, but if they could find happiness together, no matter what their age or the circumstances were, then more power to them.

"Thank you," Margie answered. She was beaming like a teenager, and Hank looked pretty pleased with himself as well.

"Why pull the trigger all of a sudden?" Moose asked. "It strikes me as odd that you'd take off with your shop's ownership in question like that."

Hank shrugged. "Margie talked to Howard Lance right before we left. There was no reason to stay."

That agreed with what we'd heard earlier about Margie being spotted with the murder victim, but I decided to keep that to myself for now.

Hank continued, "Honestly, her chat with him was kind of what started the whole thing. I realized that I'd put too much of my life into that place, turning it into some kind of shrine in Sally's memory. I loved my wife more than life itself, and if I could have changed places with her I would have done it in a heartbeat, but I couldn't, not then, and not now. It's time to move on, and that means being with Margie. Whatever happens with the clothes store happens, and we'll deal with it then." He grabbed his bride's hand and squeezed it tightly.

Margie had no comment other than to look up at her new husband with the same dopey grin I got sometimes when I looked at Greg. I had a hunch that those two crazy kids just might make it.

"Let's go, Margie. We'd better go see the sheriff and clear this up," Hank said. "We don't want anything hanging over our heads when we're trying to make a fresh start."

I hugged her on the way out, and she whispered to me, "Victoria, I'm so happy."

"I'm glad for you," I said. "Honestly."

After they were gone, Moose said, "Well, if that doesn't beat all. I never saw that coming, and don't try to tell me that you did. I knew they'd been keeping company, but marriage? At their age? What were they thinking?"

"Tell me, Moose, what is a good age to get married in your mind?" I asked my grandfather.

He shook a finger at me and frowned. "No comment. All I'm saying is that the elopement caught me off guard."

"You know what this means, don't you?" I asked, as it suddenly hit me.

"That Hank Brewer's never going to get another quiet moment in his life, now that he's gotten himself hitched again?" Moose asked with a smile.

"I'm telling Martha you said that," I replied with a grin of my own.

"Go right ahead. We don't have any secrets."

I started to pull my cell phone out of my pocket when Moose added, "Not that there's any reason to stir the pot if we don't have to."

"Agreed," I said. "That really narrows down our list of suspects, doesn't it? Those ticket stubs clear Hank and Margie of the murder."

"Two can barely even be called a list," my grandfather said.

"We have three candidates now, the way I see it."

Moose looked surprised by my statement. "Three? I just count Bob and Cynthia. You need to check your math, sunshine."

"What if it's someone who didn't even make our list?" I asked.

"It's possible," Moose said, "but I don't think so. If it was someone else, the sheriff is going to have to catch the killer, but if we've got the murderer in our sights, we've managed to get it down to a coin flip."

"I hope we're going to try to use something based more on fact than that," I said.

He glanced at the clock. "You're free for a few hours now, right?"

"I don't come back in until eleven, when Greg gets here," I said.

"Then lose the apron and let's go grill our last two fish."

I nodded to Ellen, told her that we were leaving, and then Moose and I set out to see if we could figure out which one of our remaining suspects was actually a cold-blooded killer.

Chapter 16

"Is Bob even here today?" I asked Moose as we walked into the auto repair shop.

"I'm not sure," he said. "Victoria, I don't mean to put this the wrong way, but I need to go into the shop area alone and see if he's there. If he's not, I want to ask his guys a few questions when the boss isn't around. I don't quite know how to say this, but I've got a hunch that they'll talk a little freer to me if you're not around. It's kind of a guy thing."

"I understand," I said, knowing that Moose was probably right about this.

"Don't let it bother you, I'm sure that... Hang on. What did you just say?"

"I agreed with you, and don't act like it doesn't happen all that often. Go on, maybe you'll get lucky."

"I'll be right back," my grandfather said, ducking into the shop door before I could change my mind. I wandered around for a minute, and then walked over to Bob's office. I hoped to find out where he was if he wasn't on site. Moose and I needed to chat with him, and we might not have a lot of time left before the sheriff decided to cut off our investigation. I ducked inside and looked on Bob's desk calendar, hoping to see if he had any appointments, but the thing was a mess, and nearly impossible to decipher. As I looked around the space, I shot a few squirts of spray into my mouth. It was a habit I couldn't quite break, though my husband kept insisting that my breath was always fine. As I stared at the calendar, I could see that there were dozens of telephone numbers scrawled in different places on it, directions to four different locations, doodles and drawings of airplanes, boats, swans, a few puffy clouds, one house, and at least six different stains, only a few of which I could recognize off the top of my head. This was useless. I was about to turn and try to find Moose when I glanced at the wall. There were no empty spaces on it now. As I looked closer, I saw that Bob's receipt for his original land purchase was back in its place! I started to back out of the room to tell Moose, but then I heard a polite cough behind me.

"Can I help you with something, Victoria?" Bob asked.

I pointed to the filled space amid the frames on the wall. "I thought that was missing?"

"No, it was never really gone. Someone from the cleaning crew knocked it off, and they had the glass replaced before they brought it back."

"You must have been relieved to hear that."

He shrugged. "I figured that it would turn up sooner or later. Now, why are you here?"

I tried my best not to look guilty, though in truth I had been snooping. "Moose and I were hoping to talk to you for a second," I said, giving him my brightest smile.

Bob looked around the waiting area. "I don't see your grandfather. Where is he?"

"He's out looking for you in the shop," I answered.

Bob swore under his breath, and then said, "Didn't he read the sign? If my insurance guy catches anybody back there but my mechanics, he's going to jack up my premiums on the spot. I'll be right back," he said as he left me standing there. There wasn't much I could do but wait.

The door to the shop opened suddenly, and I saw that Bob was nearly shooing my grandfather out into the waiting room.

"You can't go back there, Moose. Not now, not ever."

"I was just making conversation with some of the guys," Moose said. "It's not like I picked up a tool and tried to fix something myself." My grandfather tried to hide his hands, but not before both Bob and I could see the fresh grease stains on them.

"You worked on a car?" Bob asked loudly. The ire was clear in his voice.

"Not really," Moose said, which meant that he had done

just that.

"That's it. You two need to take off," Bob said, his patience with us finally worn thin.

"But we haven't had a chance to ask you any more questions," I protested.

Bob was adamant, though. "I was willing to indulge the two of you before, but I have a business to run here. The only questions I'll answer from now on will be from the police."

"I've got to say, you're not very welcoming to your customers," Moose said, a hint of irritation in his voice.

Bob wasn't about to back down, though. "Funny, but you have to actually use my services to be considered a customer."

"I was thinking about bringing my truck by for a tune-up," Moose said, which all three of us knew was a big fat lie. Moose enjoyed doing his own maintenance too much to let anyone else ever touch his beloved truck.

"I'll believe it when I see it. Now scoot."

I looked at Moose, shrugged, and he winked back at me. As we were walking out of the building, he said, "Bob, I'm going to have to think long and hard before I bring it in now."

"Do me a favor and take it to Newton," Bob said. "If you need a list of mechanics, I can draw one up for you."

Once we were outside, I asked Moose, "Did you have any luck? I stalled him as long as I could." That wasn't exactly true, but Bob had caught me off-guard. If I was going to do my own investigations, I was going to have to get much better at it.

"Thanks for trying. I couldn't get much out of his employees, which isn't really all that big a surprise. I just wish there was some way we could nail down his driving alibi."

"We could see when the oil was changed the last time in his car," I said. "If it was recent enough, the mileage on it now might tell us something."

"That's a great idea," Moose said. He threw me the keys to his truck as he said, "Drive around the block a few times, and make sure that Bob sees you take off."

"How am I supposed to do that, spin your tires on the pavement?"

Moose physically winced at the thought. "There's no reason to do anything crazy, Victoria. Blowing the horn should work fine."

I couldn't believe he was even letting me behind the wheel. It must be important, whatever he was about to do. "Where are you going to be while I'm your decoy?"

"I'm going to sneak back in and see if I can get to those records."

"You're taking an awful chance, aren't you?" I asked my grandfather.

"Go big or go home," he said as he ducked behind a car and headed back toward the shop.

I got into his truck and had to move the seat up so I could even drive it. After starting it up, I honked at nothing in particular, but a woman on the road in front of me must have taken offense because she honked right back, and even added a hand gesture of her own. My, my, what was happening to our friendly little town? First murder, and now this, rudeness on the highway? I forgot it almost instantly and drove Moose's truck around for at least ten minutes. As I drove, it began to rain, just a shower at first, but then it began to pick up in its intensity. On my third lap, I found my grandfather, soaking wet from the rain, waiting for me by the stop sign in front of the shop.

"Slide over," he said as he opened the driver's side door.

"Let me at least park first," I said.

"I can handle it from here," he answered, and I had no choice but to move into the passenger seat. I hadn't had the opportunity to move the bench seat back to its original position, and Moose's chest was against the steering wheel, but it was his own fault.

"Did you have any trouble?" he asked me as he wiped a

hand through his hair.

"I should be asking you the same question. Were you able to find anything out?"

He nodded, but pursed his lips as he did so. "I didn't even have to look it up. Wayne, his head mechanic, was there, and he told me that Bob's car was due for an oil change last week, but that he hadn't gotten around to it. They don't keep logs of mileage, so it was a dead-end."

"Sorry about that," I said, deflated that we hadn't been able to prove anything one way or the other."

"Don't be glum about it," Moose said. "You thought of the idea, which was more than I was able to do. It was a great plan. You can't help it that it didn't work out. Now, on to Cynthia's."

"You're enjoying this, aren't you?" I asked my grandfather as he drove to the hair salon.

"Murder is bad for everybody's business," he said, trying not to sound so happy about it.

"I know that it is, but digging into this isn't the worst thing you've ever had to do in your life, is it?"

"I do like the puzzle aspects of it," Moose admitted. "It will feel good if we can catch the killer and bring whoever it is to justice."

"Except we're calling the sheriff first thing when we figure it out, remember?"

"I'm not likely to forget it," he said. "Just because one of our witnesses turned out to be a bust doesn't mean that the other one has to."

"I saw something interesting in Bob's office," I said, mostly just to be making conversation.

Moose was deep in thought. He glanced over at me and asked, "Yeah? What was that?"

"Bob's bill of sale was back on his wall. He said someone from the cleaning crew knocked the frame off the wall, and they didn't bring it back until they could get the glass replaced. That's one loose end tied up."

I wasn't even certain that he even heard me when Moose

glanced over at me and said, "Victoria, you're about due for a new hairstyle, aren't you?"

"No, I'm happy just the way it is," I said, subconsciously pulling at my ponytail.

"Are you sure you wouldn't like to freshen your look up some?"

"Moose, I know what you're getting at, and you can just forget it. I'm not letting Cynthia touch my hair, especially not now."

"Why now in particular?" Moose asked as he pulled up in her parking lot.

"Would you like a possible murderer waving a pair of sharp cutting shears around your throat?" I asked.

"That's a good point," he conceded. "I just thought it might put her at ease if you were in the chair."

"You can do it yourself, it you're that keen on it. She does men's hair, too, you know."

He laughed. "Not even if it helped us solve this case. Lester Davenport might not have as steady a hand as he once did, but my barber does just fine by me."

I personally thought he was crazy. Since Lester had hit eighty, I had a hunch that my grandfather was in danger every time he got his hair cut.

"So, we go in and start quizzing her again right off the bat," I said.

"Unless you've got a better plan," he answered.

"I'm sorry to say that I don't," I replied as we got out of his pickup and headed for the front door. The rain had let up for the moment, but from the darkening skies, it didn't appear that would be the case for very long.

"Cynthia, do you have a second?" I asked her as Moose and I walked into the hair salon. No one else was there, and I was happy that my grandfather and I were the only visitors.

"I'm really busy," she said as she flitted about straightening magazines and making sure that everything was just so.

"This won't take long," Moose said. "It's about Howard Lance."

She accidently knocked a few magazines off one of the tables at the sound of the murder victim's name, and as she hurried to pick them up, she said, "You know what? I'm sick of talking about that man. I've told you both all that I can. Why don't you go bother Bob Chastain? He can't find his receipt, either. It was hanging on the wall before, and now it's gone. He had just as much reason to want to see something happen to that man as I did."

"We just left him there. As a matter of fact, it turns out that his receipt was just misplaced all along," I said. "Now it's your turn." I tried to add my friendliest smile so she wouldn't feel so intimidated by the barrage of questions. It was too bad I hadn't made Moose stay out in his truck for this interview, too. He could be threatening without meaning to when he failed to smile, and there was no sign of his trademark grin at the moment.

Cynthia shook her head, and then swiped at her cheek for a moment. "Fine, I'll talk. Just let me turn off something in the back. I don't want to set the place on fire."

I nodded, hoping that she'd keep the door open, but apparently she didn't want an audience. As we waited for her, Moose asked, "Did she seem particularly jumpy to you, too?"

"She's always been a bit flighty, you know that," I said.

"I realize that, but there's something more to it than that. I think if we put just a little more pressure on her, she's going to crack."

"Do you honestly want her to have a breakdown because of us?" I asked my grandfather.

"I didn't mean it that way, Victoria, but I do believe that she's about to confess."

I looked at Moose to see if he could possibly be joking, but he was deadly serious. "Do you really think she did it?"

"Why else would she be acting so guilty? She called you at the diner for information about the case, didn't she?"

I admitted as much, and Moose continued, "So, don't you think it's more than a little suspicious that she won't talk to us now? What's changed between now and then? Is her guilty conscience finally catching up with her, or is she afraid that we are hot on her trail?"

"Lower your voice, Moose," I said. "We don't want her to hear us."

"She closed the door. How's she going to do that?" Moose looked at the door she'd exited through, and then asked, "What's keeping her? Surely she's had time to turn off whatever was on back there."

Moose put a hand on the door, but I tried to stop him. "What is she going to think if we just barge in without even knocking?"

He smiled at me, knocked once, and then opened the door. "We did no such thing. See? I just knocked."

I was about to apologize to Cynthia when I noticed that the back door to the building itself was standing wide open, and her car was gone.

"Where did she go?" I asked Moose, but he was already on his phone.

"Sheriff? It's Moose. Cynthia Wilson is on the run. What? Victoria and I dropped by the salon to ask her a few questions, and she dodged out the back when we started pressing her." There was a pause, and then Moose said, "I want to go, too. Okay, that's fine. She'll understand. Bye."

"What was that all about?" I asked, even though I had a creeping suspicion that I already knew. "Sheriff Croft is swinging by here to pick me up so we can chase her down," he admitted.

"What about me?" I asked.

"He'll only let one of us go with him," Moose said. "I'm sorry, Victoria."

"That's fine. Just be careful." I knew there was no use trying to argue with him about it. It was clear that my grandfather had already made up his mind.

I walked out onto the porch with him as the rain

intensified. If my grandfather noticed it, he didn't comment. Moose handed me the keys to his truck for the second time that day, a record as far as I knew. "Don't speed on the way home."

"Don't worry. Your truck's in good hands with me. I'll try not to wreck it."

He winced a little, but he didn't reply to my comment. The sheriff was there in less than two minutes, and as Moose ran to the squad car through the rain, I waved to the sheriff, but either he didn't see me, or he chose not to respond.

After they were both gone, I wondered what I should do about the hair salon. If I left it as it was, I was afraid that someone might walk in and start taking things, though I wasn't exactly sure that there was anything of real value there. I finally decided to turn off the lights, flip the OPEN sign to CLOSED, and push the lock button as I walked out. It wasn't the same as dead-bolting the door, but I didn't have a key, and at least this would discourage an honest thief. I tried to wrap my head around the idea that Cynthia was the killer. True, she'd been jumpy about Howard Lance from the start, but that didn't necessarily make her a murderer. Why had she run, though? Most likely Moose was right, and he and the sheriff were in hot pursuit. There was nothing for me to do but drive back to the diner and see if I could lend a hand there.

As I drove back to The Charming Moose, the rain really picked up, coming down in sheets as I tried to see the road ahead of me. I'd taken a shortcut to get there, cutting past a few empty lots that were heavily wooded along the way. That was one of the things I loved about Jasper Fork. Though it was a bustling community with plenty of businesses and residences, a part of it was still untamed.

The rain was getting worse by the second, with lightning flashes quickly followed by peals of thunder, and I wasn't that familiar with Moose's truck. I decided that the best thing to do was pull over and wait it out. No one was expecting me anywhere, so it wasn't as though anybody would have reason to be worried about me. I looked for the emergency flashers on Moose's truck, but it was so old that apparently it didn't have any. Putting the park lights on instead, I shut off the engine and listened to the rain as it hammered down on the roof and the hood of the truck. It was so loud, I could barely hear myself think. How long was this downpour going to last? As I sat there watching it come down in sheets, I thought about Cynthia, and suddenly I had a hunch that Moose and the sheriff were wrong. Sure, she had motive, there was no doubt about that, but then so did Bob Chastain. While Cynthia was in full panic mode, Bob had been unusually blasé about the whole thing. The trouble was, I had a hard time believing that either one of them had the coldhearted ability to hit a man from behind and kill him while he was bending over to tie a shoe. When I considered the nature of the crime, I wondered how someone could follow Howard Lance into our diner, and then our freezer, while Greg and I had been eating less than twenty feet away. It seemed less and less likely that Cynthia could ever do that, no matter what her motivation might be.

But Bob could. I realized at that moment that I'd discounted something important worth considering. It wasn't just the opportunity to commit a crime. It was also the disposition. If Howard Lance had been poisoned, I would have had no trouble believing that Cynthia might have done it, but this was a death blow delivered while the victim's back had been turned. How hard did you have to hit someone to kill him? And how about that framed receipt that had 'suddenly' reappeared on his wall? Was his story about the cleaner true, or had Bob recovered the document from his victim, and displayed it proudly as a trophy of what he'd done?

As I began to think more about Bob, I realized something that had been staring openly at me for quite some time.

Repeated over and over again on his calendar had been figures of swans, and swans had chased me in my nightmares, along with those nasty flaming skulls. It had taken me some time to put it all together, but I finally knew that I had him. I doubted that it would be proof enough to convict him, or maybe even arrest him, but it was telling enough. I pulled out my cell phone, but the storm was so bad at first that I couldn't get any service from where I was sitting. "Moose? Are you there? Can you hear me?"

"What... you... rain." I could barely hear my grandfather, and suddenly, we were completely cut off.

Maybe it was just Moose's phone, so I called Greg at the diner. "Greg?"

"Victoria? Where are you?" There was static, but not nearly as bad as it had been with Moose.

"I'm on Briar Road," I said.

"What? I can't hear you," Greg said, and the coverage dropped off almost completely after that.

"Briar Road!" I shouted, but when I looked again, the phone was dead. I wasn't sure if lightning had hit a tower, or if the rain had ruined my reception, but I knew that I was on my own.

That meant that, storm or no storm, I was going to have to drive somewhere and tell the police why I suspected that Bob Chastain was a cold-blooded killer.

I started the truck engine and then began to pull out when I felt a crushing jolt from just behind me, ramming me into an oak tree. Someone had hit Moose's truck in the storm, and pinned me in the driver's seat!

The seatbelt had locked with the impact from the other vehicle, and I pounded on the release latch trying to get it to open, but it wouldn't even budge. I looked around wildly for something to use as a weapon, but there wasn't anything there except my cell phone and a handbag with nothing more lethal in it than breath spray. Could I use that? I held on tight as I looked through the rain and saw lightning flashing, cutting through the temporary darkness. In that moment, I'd seen Bob walking toward me, a wicked smile on his face as he pressed on. It was as though he didn't even feel the onslaught of the weather all around him. To anyone driving by, it would most likely look as though Bob was just being a Good Samaritan.

They would be wrong, but would anyone realize it in time to do me any good?

Bob tapped on my window, and I had no choice but to lower it.

One look at my face told him all that he needed to know. As he grinned, the rain dripped down his face. "You figured it out, didn't you? I don't know how, but you always were the clever one. Get out of the truck, Victoria."

"I can't," I said.

"Can't, or won't?" he asked.

"The seatbelt is jammed shut," I said.

As he leaned over to try to free it himself, I shot him in the eyes with the mouth spray. He reeled back, rubbing his eyes to ease the pain he had to be feeling, and I swung at him as hard as I could with my cell phone in my hand.

It glanced off him and fell into the mud at his feet.

As he tried to clear his eyes, I struggled again with the seatbelt. Why wouldn't it release? If I sat there too long, I was going to die, and I knew it.

Summoning up all the energy that I had, I pounded on it, and then, with the suddenness of a kick in the stomach, it released, and I was free.

I struggled to open the passenger side door as Bob roared in anger and frustration. I was certain he was displeased with my failure to just sit there like a good little victim, but I had other plans. Throwing open the door, I stumbled out into the storm, knowing that it was my only chance.

And then my feet hit a gulley, and sweeping water washed my legs out from under me.

As I struggled to get to my feet, I felt a pair of strong hands driving me back into the water and the mud.

He was too strong for me.

As I tried to get up again, Bob drove me back down. He placed his knees on my chest, and I was helpless. The only thing that I could do was try to stay alive long enough for help to arrive.

"There's just one thing I need to know before we're finished here," Bob said. "How did you figure it out?"

"I suspected it when you didn't seem all that upset that your receipt had been stolen off the wall of your office, and it was too much of a coincidence when it suddenly reappeared, but I didn't know for sure until I remembered what I'd seen on your calendar."

Bob looked honestly surprised by that. "You're joking. There was nothing incriminating there. I wouldn't be that stupid."

I thought of a quick insult, but decided to keep it to myself. The only question now was should I tell him the truth, or should I lie? If I kept the knowledge from him, maybe the sheriff would be able to figure it out himself.

And then I realized that without my specialized knowledge of the case, no one would be able to put the two things together but Greg, and he wasn't investigating the murder.

I was still mulling over my options when Bob's knees forced me deeper into the rising water. Was I going to drown in ten inches of water? "You'd better hurry up, Victoria. You're running out of time," he said.

"It was the swans," I said.

"What are you talking about?"

"No one knew that we were stowing an ice sculpture in our freezer the day you murdered Howard Lance. Your drawings looked much more like the sculpture than actual swans, so I knew that you'd been in that freezer at the time of the murder."

"Well, I'll be. I never even realized what I was doing," he said. "Don't you worry, though. I'll take care of that as soon as I get back to my office."

"I told you the truth," I said as some water slipped into my mouth. I choked on the brown filthy sludge, and spit most of it out. "The least you can do is come clean with me."

"I'm afraid your days of being clean are over," he said, chuckling a little as he did. Bob looked around, but evidently, no one else was out braving the elements in the middle of this storm, at least not on the shortcut I'd taken.

"It will have to be quick, but I'll give you the highlights. Howard Lance came to me first with his little extortion plot, and I immediately saw it for the opportunity it was. He was a bit of a bungler, but I convinced him that I'd figure out a way to make us both rich."

"Is the auto repair business that bad?" I asked him.

"It's okay, but it's never been enough, you know? Anyway, Howard decided to get cute and double-cross me. He stole my own receipt from my office, and told me I wouldn't get it back until we finished our business arrangement. Cynthia paid up, but everybody else was being a lot more stubborn than she was. It was falling apart fast, so I figured out that the only person who could link me to the mess was Howard himself. He had to go, and after I took care of him, I reclaimed what was rightfully mine. The money was already gone, though." Bob seemed particularly unhappy about that development.

"But why kill him at our diner?" I asked. Was that the sound of water rushing toward us? I knew that gullies could fill up quickly during storms, and this was turning out to be a doozy. Maybe it would be strong enough to sweep Bob away as well. That was the only way I was going to have a fighting chance.

"I was going to kill him in the alley to make you all look guilty, but just before he got there for our little 'meeting,' I checked the back door on a whim and found that it was unlocked. When Howard showed up, I told him that I'd found the real receipt for the diner inside, and that if we had that, we'd own you people. He believed me, and when I peeked inside, the kitchen was deserted. I lured him into the freezer, mostly so we'd be out of sight from the cursed window pass-through. At first I was going to lock him in and be done with it, but who knows how long it would have taken him to freeze to death? It was too risky, so when Howard leaned forward to look for your receipt, I took care of him."

"That was an awfully big risk," I said as the rushing water grew louder.

"Hey, I did what I had to do. Anyway, that's it. I'm sorry to have to do this, Victoria. I've always liked you, but this just can't be helped."

I fought him with the last bit of energy I had, but he had his full weight on me, and the positioning made it impossible for me to fight back.

It looked as though I was about to die.

Chapter 17

I wasn't just going to give up, though, no matter how hopeless the situation seemed to be. With everything I had left, I struggled to hold my head above the water around me. I wasn't fighting Bob anymore. I was struggling against the rising water.

Steadily, resolutely, almost as though it were all happening in slow motion, my head went lower and lower into the water. My ears were under, and as it crept up my cheeks toward my nose and mouth, the sounds around me took on a surreal feel, as though the world was being muted.

And then, as suddenly as a lightning strike, Bob's full weight was off me and I was able to raise my head again. It was disorienting at first, but I finally managed to sit up when I heard Greg's voice as he held my head against his chest.

"You're going to be all right," he said softly, rocking me against his chest.

"I got through on the phone after all?"

"It took me a few minutes to figure out that you were saying Briar Road," Greg admitted. "I called the sheriff's office, and they patched me through to him and Moose. We got here at nearly the same time. Moose and the sheriff took care of Bob, so I could get to you. Did he hurt you?"

I felt the bruising on my shoulders and chest where his knees had pinned me down, and the water still in my ears. My back ached from the impact on the ground, and my stomach was strained from where the seatbelt had bitten into me.

But I was still alive, and that was more than I had any right to expect.

"You know what? I've never been better in my entire life," I said as I hugged him fiercely.

"Let's get you up and out of here," Moose said.

"We'd better wait for the paramedics," Sheriff Croft said as he put one hand on my shoulder.

"What do you think, Victoria?" Greg asked me softly.

"Better safe than sorry," I said as I heard the sirens of the ambulance coming closer. Honestly, I wasn't sure if I could even stand with the help of three strong men there. "I don't know what I would have done without you all," I said.

"I'm just glad you didn't have to find out," Greg said, stroking my muddy hair.

The sheriff knelt down and said softly, "I owe you one, Victoria. You managed to hang on until we got here, and you figured this entire mess out before I did."

"That's because you didn't have all the clues that I did."

"You weren't holding back on me, were you?" he asked as he looked sternly at me.

I shook my head slightly, and that's when I felt a major headache coming on. "Let me ask you something, Sheriff. Would you have known what drawings of swans meant?"

"Swans? No, I don't have any idea what you're talking about. Did you hit your head when you went down?"

Greg got it, though, and almost immediately. "Bob was in the freezer. That's the only way he would have seen the ice sculpture, and that's how you figured out that he had to be the killer."

"I knew there was a reason I married you," I said with a smile.

"You mean you love me for my mind and not my rugged good looks?" he asked, grinning down at me.

"Let's just say that I went for the package deal," I said.

"Victoria, I need to get a statement from you, the sooner the better," the sheriff said as the EMTs approached.

"Can it wait until she gets checked out first?" Moose asked.

The sheriff looked at me, and then at my husband. "That will be fine. You coming with me, Moose? There's only going to be room for the two of them in the ambulance."

"In a second," he said, and then turned back to me.

"I'm so sorry about your truck," I said. "How bad is it?"

"Oh, it's completely totaled," he said with a dismayingly broad grin.

"I thought you'd be upset," I said.

"Victoria, you're more important to me than a thousand trucks, and a hundred diners, all of them with my name on them. I love you, kiddo."

"I love you, too," I said.

That was about all the time I had for conversation as the EMTs moved in and got me strapped to a stretcher. I thought that it was a bit of overkill, but I wasn't exactly in a position to refuse the attention.

I wasn't sure which felt better, finishing the rigorous exam and finally being able to clean myself up, or being surrounded by my family. Dad nearly cracked my ribs when he hugged me, and Martha wouldn't stop crying, even after learning that I was safe.

Then, something occurred to me. "If you're all here, who's running the diner? Surely you didn't leave it in Ellen and Jenny's hands."

"We shut the place down for the rest of the day," Greg said.

I sat up on the examining room bed, wearing the scrubs the hospital had loaned me, and looked at my family. "As much as I love you all being here, you've completely lost your minds. Go back and open up. I'm fine."

"Can I at least stay here with you?" Greg asked.

I was about to speak when Moose said, "Sure you can. I've been itching to get back on the grill for a while now." He looked at my dad. "What do you say, son? Care to lend me a hand?"

"I'd like that," he said, and I watched with delight as Moose put his arm around his son.

"What about me?" my mother asked. "I like to cook, too."

"All three of us will do it," Moose said with a booming

laugh.

"I'll take the register," Martha said, and we were all surprised yet again by her willingness to return to her former duties at the diner.

"Then let's stop lollygagging around here and get back to work," Moose said.

They each took turns saying goodbye, and after they were gone and I'd given my statement to Sheriff Croft, Greg asked, "Are you ready to go home?"

I nodded as they made me get into a wheelchair before they'd allow me to leave. "I want to grab a quick shower and change, and then I'd like to go back to the diner, if you wouldn't mind."

"Mind? I doubt I could keep you from the place even if I tried."

I touched his hand lightly as I said, "You understand, don't you?"

"Hey, home is where the heart is," Greg said, "and for us, that's The Charming Moose."

And that, among a thousand other reasons, was why I loved my husband as much as I did.

Home, The Charming Moose, was exactly where I needed to be.

If you enjoyed A Chili Death, be sure to try the next in the series,

A Bad Beef, COMING SOON!

Chapter 1

It's important to understand that we had to fire Wally Bain, and if that made us suspects when he was murdered the next day, we had no way of knowing it at the time. The Charming Moose prided itself on providing good diner food at a fair price to the folks of Jasper Fork, North Carolina, and Wally had not lived up to his part of the bargain in supplying us with fresh fruits and vegetables from his farm when they were in season.

Sheriff Croft had that 'tough lawman' look on his face when he walked into The Charming Moose. Dressed in his police uniform, he took off his cap as soon as he came in.

"Victoria, I need to know about the fight you had with Wally Bain yesterday."

"What happened, did he come crying to you about it?" I asked. "You should have seen the last load of spinach he brought us. It was wormy!" The season for Wally's supply schedule was just about finished, and we hadn't been happy with his offerings for months. We were on a yearly contract with him, and this delivery had been the last straw.

"So, did you fire him?"

"Technically, we told him that we weren't renewing his contract for next season, but yeah, we fired him."

"How'd he take it?" the sheriff asked.

"About what you'd expect from him," I said. "He wasn't happy about it, and when he started yelling at me, Greg and Moose came running."

"So, the three of you ganged up on him?"

What was the sheriff's problem today? He was on edge, something that usually couldn't be used to describe him. "Is he saying someone hit him? We never laid a finger on the man, and if he told you otherwise, he's a liar. Bring him in here, and I'll say that to his face."

"I'm sorry to say that I can't do that," the sheriff said. "Someone murdered him on his farm sometime between midnight and noon."

Made in the USA
Lexington, KY
23 September 2013